RESCUE SOMEONE LONESOME

A SWEET GARDNER RANCH WESTERN ROMANCE

BRITTNI MINER

EBURNEAN
BOOKS

RESCUE SOMEONE LONESOME

For Paige and Kenny, because an acknowledgement doesn't feel like it would be enough. You two have changed my writing.

GET A FREE NOVELLA

Want more sweet romance?

Get a copy of Brittni's swoon-worthy novella, Call It Kismet, for free!

Get my book!

PROLOGUE

The wind picked up, whipping locks of hair loose from Raquel's ponytail. She pulled her cardigan tight around her shoulders and squinted her eyes in a desperate attempt to keep dust out. The trees lining the front drive were alive with the gale, their thin leaves quivering. They made a soft, rustling noise as they shook, like tiny wings flapping.

She wasn't sure she could help Adam as he worked out in the storm—not with the way that he looked now. Raquel could hardly see him through the dust and rain, but what she did see made her pause in wonder. His blonde hair had been smoothed down like a sheet against his skin, hugging jutting cheekbones and sharp jawline. His shirt, too, clung to his body, making him appear slick and lithe. In the downpour, Adam almost presented as one of the horses he was corralling: something primal and brute.

Terrifying to behold. Impossible to ignore.

ONE

SWEAT. Numbness. Nausea.

Raquel Villanueva had her first ever panic attack in the frozen foods section of the grocery store.

It took her by surprise. There wasn't any buildup to it like she'd seen in the soaps her Mama used to play for her grandparents before her abuela passed away. She didn't feel herself going light-headed. The world didn't go dark and fuzzy at the edges. There was no time to scream for someone to bring the smelling salts.

Raquel had been trying to decide between chocolate chip or rocky road ice cream. She'd reached for the handle of the freezer and *boom*. In one lightning-fast second, she was doubled over, white-knuckling a pint of Ben and Jerry's before slamming it to a creamy explosion on the grocery store tile.

Headache. Fingers tingling. Heart pounding.

There was a weight on her chest. It was invisible, but monumental. It pressed against her lungs, forcing them to expand vertically instead of their intended horizontal.

Raquel fell to all fours, the ruptured pint of ice cream forgotten as she tried to remember how to breathe.

A stock boy had reached her first.

"Are you okay, miss?"

He peered over the rim of thick, tortoise-shell glasses, his question dripping out slower than molasses. She struggled to hear him over the echoing sounds of the grocery store's Top 100 playlist, which had Train's *Drops of Jupiter* playing at an obnoxious volume.

Raquel shook her head and clutched at her button-down shirt, as though the action might make breathing easier.

"Help..." she croaked, her voice catching with each desperate inhale.

Even in the midst of medical crisis, she had to will back the blush that she knew must be overtaking her cheeks. And it took a *lot* to make a Latina girl look like she was blushing.

The teen pulled her up by her elbows, and she collapsed into his side. He smelled like Mountain Dew and tobacco. The sour-sweet combination made the grocery store tile rush up at her all over again, and Raquel clutched at his work apron. He gently guided her towards the front of the store, but she could barely concentrate as the world spun around her.

"You want me to go back for your ice cream, miss?" he asked.

She pictured the explosion of cream and marshmallow by the freezer and shook her head. "I'm good," she croaked. "Peachy. You can get back to work, really."

He sat her down on a wooden bench by the doors. By this point, people were rubbernecking. Raquel felt her own neck retreating under her collar. She was a turtle in desperate need of its shell.

"I can just go," Raquel assured the stock boy. More sweat. More nausea. More tingling in the tips of her fingers. Her heart pounded faster in her chest, making her feel all the more desperate to get rid of this lingering stock boy.

"I'm fine," Raquel insisted. Her still-ragged breathing caught on the last words, and she cursed in her head.

"Your cart is still back there, miss—" he started.

She waved him off. "I'll make another trip."

"I could get in trouble, miss—" he stammered.

"Seriously—"

"Miss—"

"Call me miss one more time."

She shot him a *look*. Her own forcefulness surprised her.

It was a testament to just how badly she needed to get out of that grocery store: Raquel wasn't the kind of girl who took charge of a situation. She certainly wasn't the kind to stare down insistent stock boys. But right now, with her arms covered in melty ice cream and a crowd full of shoppers still trying to catch a glimpse of the frozen foods fiasco, she felt more than prepared to take him on.

She'd always been more introverted, but she had never been this outright scared and stuttering. She couldn't allow herself to slip into that now, anxiety attack or not. Raquel jutted out her chin, doing her best imitation of her fierce, self-confident Latin mother.

The boy's gulp was visible as he nodded in her direction. "Ok, miss," he said. His face whitened as he realized what word he had repeated. "Um, are you sure—"

"I'm *sure*." Raquel stood up and headed for the automatic doors as fast as she could. Ah, *there* were those fuzzy edges she'd seen in the movies. *There* was the light-headed feeling. She did her best to ignore it all as she navigated the parking lot for her tiny Camry, her delicate kitten heels clacking out each careful step.

The unforgiving Las Vegas sun didn't help the way that she felt. She pulled open her door and only just made it to collapse in the car before the spinning, the sweat, and—worst of all—the *feelings* all became too much for her. She turned on her car and blasted the air conditioning. She rested her face against the tiny air vent, letting the gust freeze the tears she could feel starting to roll.

Raquel might be too emotional, but she wasn't an idiot. She knew why the panic attack had come on. It had been the stupid ice cream.

She couldn't remember the last time that she'd had to choose between ice cream flavors. She'd always let Jude choose before. He had preferences, moods. One time he'd gotten a wild hair for the perfect banana split, and Raquel had spent a Sunday with him driving three cities over to find the right brand of whipped cream.

And the moods were for everything, not just ice cream. In fact, Jude having the stronger, more quirky personality was part of what made Raquel feel like they were a good match. They were a complement, a pretty pair. When they introduced themselves as a couple, friends and strangers loved to tout the phrase "opposites attract." Raquel had clung to that. A couple like her and Jude were supposed to work. Right?

So over the three years they'd been together, Raquel had gotten good at predicting Jude's tastes and inclinations. There was comfort in them. A predictability, even in the unpredictable. Jude would bring her some treat home and she never had to give the purchase a second thought.

Raquel shook her head now, closing her eyes tight. Even

with every ounce of her energy diverted to distracting herself, Raquel's mind had wandered back to the great forbidden place, to the eye of her internal ice-cream-panic-attack storm.

Was he buying ice cream for Abby now? It was probably the good stuff, too, like the Häagen-Dazs he used to bring back after long work trips. They'd be eating it together in Raquel's kitchen, with Raquel's silverware. Jude would dip up two scoops for each of them and Abby would pull out the special Luxardo cherries to go on top. Raquel had given Jude the first jar of those when she'd gotten them on a family trip overseas.

Abby was so short that she'd have to pull the stepstool out of the hall closet to reach them. Raquel could see it playing out in her mind's eye. Jude, with his strong, tanned arms wrapping around Abby's slight, sloping shoulders to help her reach the cherries. Pushing aside the mass of her tightly coiled brown hair to kiss the daisy tattoo on her neck. She'd pretend not to like all that, of course: Abby had always been too independent and strong-willed for all the romance stuff. But in the end, her impulsive nature would force her to give in and her fingertips would go arching back to run through his own silky, dark waves. They'd look so perfect together: Abby with her funky, confident style and Jude with his classic good looks. Like a super model couple, living the perfect life that Raquel had built for them…

The weight was back on Raquel's chest in an instant, crushing her lungs and making her death-grip her steering wheel. She had to calm down. She had to get this under control.

Raquel told the mantra to her patients all the time: "All is well, all is well." If strung-out, impaled, or gunshot victim patients in a Vegas ER could remember six simple words, she could do it, too.

But then again, what did she know? She was only the nurse. It's not like she was an actual doctor. Raquel allowed herself a moment of banging her head against the air conditioning vent and cursing under her breath.

Her giant cell phone vibrated in her pocket, bringing her back to reality.

MOM.

She moaned and closed her eyes, her head dropping back against the driver's seat. Great. This was just what she needed right now. Raquel bit the bullet and accepted the call.

"Hi, Mama."

"Hola, lovely." Her mother's voice was as bright and breezy as it always was, but Raquel knew her well enough to sense the edge behind the words. Miriam was worried about her daughter. Her only child. The one who had just lost her boyfriend of three years to her best friend and was now having very public, very humiliating panic attacks in the middle of Vons Grocery Store.

"Did I interrupt anything special?" Miriam asked. The last word floated up at the end, a clear indicator of hope and excitement. Raquel could picture her mother cooking in the kitchen as always, one pinky wandering up to tap her bottom lip as it did when she was prying and hoping for a specific answer.

Raquel sighed. She hated being a constant letdown. She cleared her throat.

"I'm not getting ready for a date, Mama. I'm never getting ready for a date." She sighed again. How could she begin to ease her mother into letting this go? "It's really not worth asking anymore. I promise I'm trying to move on though. Really."

"Did I ask if you were getting ready for a date? Did I say those words?" Miriam's voice was dripping with innocence. Raquel could envision her with her hands in the air, even though no one but the family cat and Raquel's ancient abuelo would be home to see her.

"A mama just likes to check on her daughter is all," Miriam went on. "Although if you did have a handsome man chasing after you, it wouldn't be the end of the world..."

"Mama."

"You're nearing thirty. The women in my book club have started asking if you'll just move in with me and abuelo now that Jude is gone as our retirement nurse."

"*Mama, please.*" Raquel swallowed darn a sharp intake of breath as she tried to sound firm and resolute. Her plea came out sounding less confident and more desperate.

"Right, right," Miriam huffed. She paused for a moment, and Raquel could hear her deep, steady breaths. She was refocusing, altering her approach.

Her mother was the stereotypical matchmaker, but she did have her daughter's best interests at heart. The night that Jude and Abby had sat Raquel down to talk with her together for the first time, Miriam had shown up within the hour bearing wine and chocolates and swearing up and down that she would neuter that boy if she ever saw him in person again. She wouldn't let her desire for grandchildren outweigh her desire for her daughter's happiness.

"Believe it or not, I really didn't call to hound you about your dating life," Miriam assured her. "I called with a job opportunity. There's a nice, single man out in Arizona—"

"A job opportunity?" Raquel rubbed at her eyes. "Mama,

I'm up for a promotion at the hospital. It should be, like, any day now."

"Yes, well, as likely as I think you are to find your husband wearing the pajamas and sneakers you insist on wearing to work—"

"They're called scrubs, Ma," Raquel reminded her.

"Well, I did hear of an interesting opportunity. Lila Black forwarded me the cutest message yesterday. Usually, I only forward the ones with the funny jokes or the horoscopes, but this one was different. Made me think of you."

Raquel's fingers were drumming out an impatient beat on her steering wheel. This conversation needed to wrap up, or she might start to spiral again. When Miriam got going on the life advice train, there was no getting her off. The whole process usually left Raquel feeling more unsure than when they started talking.

"I'm happy here, Mama. I really am. Jude and Abby will stick to their part of town, and I'll stick to mine. I never even have to think about them again."

But was she saying it more to remind her mother or to remind herself?

In a moment, it was as though Raquel was standing in the ice cream aisle again, her heart pounding and skin burning. She wanted to move on. She wanted to forget the sensitive, pitying, *mortifying* words that Jude and Abby had spoken to her. To erase the lingering, scorching sense of betrayal when she'd realized that her best friend—the one she had introduced to Jude, the one who she'd confided in for every personal, intimate moment with him—was the same person who stole him away from Raquel and left her alone, empty, and with no sense of who she had ever been before him.

How could she even begin to move on when she didn't

know what to move on to? When she didn't know what she wanted at all?

"I'll see you at home, Mama." Her voice was strangled.

"I'm volunteering at the church this evening," Miriam explained. "I leave in a few, and I'll miss you. Just take a look at your email account, okay? I know it sounds silly to you. But I think this might just be what you need."

"Sure," Raquel agreed. "I'll look."

"And your abuelo has his bridge game tonight, don't forget. He'll need a lift."

"Of course, Ma. Bye."

Raquel hung up the phone and pushed in the antenna. What was the point in putting up all that money to purchase a cell phone when the only calls she got were from her overbearing mother?

Nevertheless, she couldn't help but feel a little touched by the gesture. She would take a look at the job opportunity. For her mama.

On instinct, Raquel started to dial a familiar number. The only other number besides Jude's or her mother's that she had ever used the phone to call before. She stopped, sitting on her hands for fear that they might dial without her permission. That option was gone. Just like Jude, there was no getting it back. Her chest ached.

She took down the elastic of her ponytail, running her fingers through the loose, black waves. She rubbed at her scalp, scratching at it like she could scrape off every lingering memory of the past two months.

Raquel felt very sure that a new job wouldn't be the solution to her problems. A new job out in Arizona wouldn't repair her broken relationship. A new job wouldn't erase the hurt and the embarrassment. And it wouldn't prevent this new sense of panic she got every time that she was faced with making her own decisions or taking charge of her own life.

Worst of all, she hadn't even gotten the opportunity to pick out an ice cream back at the grocery store. How was she supposed to drown her sorrows now?

TWO

AFTER SHE READ THE EMAIL, Raquel understood why her mother had been so insistent she open it.

She had returned home from the grocery store, poked her head in to her abuelo's bedroom to wave hello, and booted up the computer. As the dial-up scratched and squealed, she wandered over to the freezer in the kitchen, opening it up and feeling more than a little disappointed when she discovered that the only ice cream her mother had was Rum Raisin. Even at her most indecisive, she knew that she couldn't stomach that. After several minutes had passed and the desktop had been given a chance to breathe, she headed over and pulled up her email.

As per usual, Raquel's Outlook was near-empty and meticulously organized. The message was impossible to miss. Even if she had emails from anyone else—she didn't—she still would have noticed the subject line: *Pretty, Single Nurse Wanted*. No wonder her mother had been so quick to forward it over.

Raquel clicked on the message, suppressing the massive

sigh she could feel building up in her chest. A flashy text in bright purple font appeared.

Are you a young, single, attractive nurse? Are you interested in physically impaired but also unreasonably charming 27-year-old men? Have we got the job for you! Come to quaint Goldfinch, Arizona, where you'll have free housing and meals on top of a generous salary. Come for the money, stay for your charge's self-deprecating handicap jokes and rugged country good looks. Brunettes with brown eyes preferred. Must love bad sci-fi movies and junk food. Courteney Cox look-a-likes need not apply.

Raquel couldn't help it: she snorted. Was this ad for real? It had to be one of those fake forwards Miriam was always sending around, lest she be cursed with bad fortune for seven years.

She scrolled down. There was a video clip attached at the bottom for "proof of cowboy charm." And there was an actual phone number listed for contact. Jeez, this guy must be desperate to find his beautiful brunette nurse—but only as long as she didn't look too much like Courteney Cox. Talk about picky.

Raquel's phone went off in her purse. She pulled it out, stretching out the antenna as she opened it.

"Very funny, Mama," she said, propping her heeled feet up next to the desktop.

"Funny? I'm serious!"

Raquel could hear the noises of a busy church gym in the background. "Are you really calling me from the volunteer activity to make sure I read your forward? This help-wanted ad feels dangerously close to a mail-order bride blurb."

"It sounds like a good job, Mija," her mother insisted. "A comfortable salary? Free housing and meals? And the client is good-looking!"

"He *claims* to be good-looking," Raquel reminded her. "That's different. He also sounds pretty darn full of himself."

"Raquel Maria Garcia Villanueva, there are only so many times I can light a prayer candle for you. Jude broke up with you four months ago. It's time to move on."

Raquel dropped her feet from their resting spot on the counter. "Jeez."

"Mija, *he's engaged.*"

And there it was. The great big thing that Raquel had banned either her mother or grandfather from bringing up.

Jude had proposed to Abby the weekend before. Las Vegas was a big town, but their circle was small. Raquel had heard about it from three different people the night it happened. It had taken Jude less than four months to pop the question that Raquel had waited three years to hear. She had food in her mother's fridge that was older than that.

The one and only fight that Raquel had with her mother after moving back home had been about the engagement. *Why didn't you ask him yourself? Maybe then you would have him locked down.* Miriam hadn't meant for the words to sting as hard as they had. She had been trying to encourage her daughter to take charge and learn from her mistakes for next time. But the truth hurt Raquel. It hurt her pride just as much as it hurt her heart.

Raquel had heard from mutual friends that Abby and Jude wanted to get married before the end of the year: a short engagement to match a short courtship. It was hard for Raquel to envision them going through with it though. Even though she knew she wasn't the type to interrupt a wedding at "Speak now or hold your peace" or even the kind of girl who would so much as approach Jude for a reconciliation, she was still holding out some kind of hope that this whole debacle would just... disappear.

Engagements ended all the time. So that's what Raquel kept repeating to herself, never saying the words out loud so that no one could contradict her. *Engagements end all the time, all the time, all the time.* It was far preferable to facing her sense of loss, or loneliness, or crushing panic. Because if she did that, she might just find herself under that last, heavy rock from which she couldn't scratch her way out. The shy, timid introvert would go full hopeless hermit, all sense of hope or confidence dashed forever.

Raquel knew it was extreme to think this way. But she also knew how she felt when she was on the floor of Vons frozen foods aisle, clutching at her shirt collar as she fought for a deep breath.

"I'm not going after this new job, Mama," she declared. Miriam started to cut off her daughter, but Raquel persisted. "I'm going to figure this out. I'm going to move on. I don't need some backwoods, country western cocky ranch boy to get me out of my slump. I need your support."

Her mother sighed. The sound crackled over the line. "You will always have that. Forget I sent the forward."

Raquel nodded. "You can get back to the church now," she said. "I'm sure that Father Pete is lost without your organization."

"Of course, he is." Raquel could hear the smile in her Mama's voice. She'd bridged the gap between them. Raquel turned off the phone.

As when she hung up with her mother before, she was left tired and shaky. She glanced up at the help-wanted ad still pulled up on her email.

She could see why this message had turned into a popular forward. She could imagine the self-assured, vain son-of-a-gun who had written the email, sure, but she could also see the humor in it. She'd never cared much for Courteney Cox herself, and she had thought that maybe she was one of the only people on Earth who didn't find all of the *Friends* cast attractive. And she did love terrible sci-fi movies. The higher the sequel number, the better.

She was young. She was single. And Jude had considered her pretty at one point, even if he had ultimately decided that he thought her best friend was prettier. Maybe in another life, she could have been this rancher's mail-order nurse.

Raquel hovered her mouse over the video link and clicked. A grainy clip filled the screen of a tall cowboy mounted on a horse, riding fast through the weeds of an overgrown field. She had to squint to make out the details. The man was blurry at best. But she could make out his smile no problem.

It was one of those snarky half-smiles, the kind that didn't quite extend to the eyes and left its recipient feeling like its owner had secrets. It seemed to Raquel that this Arizona rancher was trying his best to look happy for whoever was taking the video, but he couldn't quite give the emotion his all. It was a feeling she felt resonating inside of her own self, leaving her both troubled and surprisingly intrigued.

Raquel exited out of her email and powered down the desktop. Maybe it could have been. But not this time.

"Mija?" Her abuelo's low, crackly voice called to her from a nearby bedroom. "Are you using the internets again? I would like to make a call to Aunt Betty, but it is not going through."

Raquel shook her head. "Sorry, abuelo. I just got off."

Her abuelo rolled into the living room, his chair

creaking across the old floorboards. "Do not let me rush you if you are busy."

He looked tired today. The purple rings were more pronounced under his eyes. His salt and pepper mop of hair was unbrushed and matted. Raquel rushed over to him, pushing his chair the rest of the way into the room.

"I'm not busy, promise." She assured him. "You can make your call in here. I was just leaving."

"Honestly, I would rather talk to you than that sour old Betty." Her abuelo smiled, exposing a mouth full of square, still pristine white teeth. "I just needed the distraction today. I—"

He winced, pawing at his left leg. Or rather, at what was left of his left leg.

Diego Villanueva had lost his leg in a military plane crash long before Raquel had ever been born. He had been fitted for a prosthetic leg years ago, but he had preferred the chair in the end. Phantom pain in his amputated limb still haunted him, and a prosthetic only enhanced the strange sensations.

The whole thing left Raquel feeling bad for him. She loved her abuelo—he was funny, charming, and always good for a thrilling story about his time serving in the Air Force. But there was something haunting about the way he spoke of his military past. He loved those planes so much and he relished his time in the air... it was hard to reconcile that nostalgia with the man doomed to be bound to his chair.

It was the reason Raquel had decided to become a nurse. If she could help anyone, even a little, maybe it would help her own strange sense of loss. It couldn't put Diego back in a plane. It couldn't get her back together with Jude, either, or help her reconcile with her best friend. But it was something. Raquel could be a fixer, the person people turned to when the life they desperately wanted didn't turn out in the end. She'd be there to pick up the pieces and show them the bright side of living a less risky life.

"You're looking at me that way again, Mija." Diego smiled wryly as he wheeled himself over to the wet bar. He pulled out a glass and held up another, gesturing for her. She waved him off, rejecting it. "I don't need your pity just because I am having an off day."

Raquel crossed her arms and smiled, leaning up against the bar as he poured himself a cold beer. "I can do more than distract you, ya know," she offered. "We can try some imagery or music. Just like the doctor suggested. Or I can schedule you an appointment with the acupuncturist?"

"Just give it some time, Raquel. The pain will subside on its own." He smiled and reached over to pat her arm. "I am not broken just because I am going through a hard time."

Raquel sighed and motioned for him to give her that glass of beer after all.

"Did your mother ask if you could take me to bridge today?" Diego asked as he poured. "There's a flight show after, if you'd like to stay."

"A flight show?"

"Down by the Strip," he nodded. "Old military planes, mostly. Interested?"

"Alright," Raquel agreed with a small smile. "It's not like I have anywhere else to be."

Her abuelo must have seen the dark flash in her eyes. He clasped his hands around her own as she took the glass of beer. "This too shall pass, Mija," he assured her. "You'll find someone else to love. You'll find peace in enjoying the ride and continuing to live your life. Take it from someone who knows."

He cleared his throat and took another swig, polishing off his glass.

"You will love some of these planes, Raquel. They have my old ride, of course, and a B-52..."

Raquel's smile grew as she listened to Diego drone on about his favorite planes. Even after all this time, after the accident, he still lived for the air.

Maybe he was right. Maybe her trauma would also pass. Raquel wasn't sure yet. But she definitely hoped that he was right—even if the last thing she needed right now was to fall in love again.

A CHEAP, shabby poster hung on the wall behind Raquel's boss.

It had bothered Raquel every time she went into Mr. Nordstrom's office. It was one of those motivational numbers, with a cat hanging from a thin tree branch. "Hang in there!" the text read. It was cutesy. A tchotchke. It didn't belong in the office of a well-regarded medical professional.

But it did fit with Mr. Nordstrom. He was an ancient, sniveling man with a penchant for hard-boiled eggs and the lingering sour breath to prove it. He ran the nurses under his charge with little supervision, but plenty of opinions. If anyone was the kind of man to give out vague, meaningless advice like "hang in there," it was someone like him. Raquel loathed having to meet with him in his office.

Nordstrom looked down over his long, hooked nose at her file.

"Your marks are good," he commented. "The patients like you. So do your shift leads. And you've been here for a long time." He peered up at her, his watery brown eyes examining her up and down. "Commitment. I like it."

"Five years," she volunteered. "I've been here since nursing school."

"Five years in the same position?" Nordstrom's eyebrows went up.

"Well, about that," Raquel started. Even having prepped to asked for what she wanted, she struggled to find the right words. "I, um... I was hoping that this quarterly review might..."

Nordstrom shut her file and placed it on his desk. He folded his leathery hands neat in front of him. "You need your hours adjusted?"

"No, sir," Raquel said. "I love my hours. In fact—"

"Vacation time, then? Need a little rest and relaxation to pump out five more years?"

"*Sir.*" She did her best to sound firm. Her voice wasn't as strong as she might have liked. Raquel cleared her throat. "I like my hours. I like my vacation time. I'm even happy with my pay. What I was hoping for was a little more...responsibility."

Just giving voice to what she wanted made Raquel feel the now-familiar panicked breathing. Her skin had grown hot and damp under her scrubs. There was a high-pitched ringing in her ears that she knew only she could hear. She did her best to sit up straight and pretend like she had all the confidence in the world.

But her hopes were dashed as soon as Nordstrom's mouth turned down the corners. It was the sympathy look. Pity.

"Rachel, we already have all the shift leads we need—"

She didn't bother to correct his irritating pronunciation of her name. Instead, she reminded herself of what she had rehearsed in her mirror prior to their meeting.

"I, um, was thinking that you might consider creating a

new position," she stammered. "We're seeing more patients than ever, and our turnover rate is through the roof."

"I tell you what," Nordstrom started. "I can raise your pay by one percent. You'll be the envy of all your coworkers." He grinned at her, like she should be overjoyed.

"But sir—"

He waved her off and started to pick up his phone to make a call. "Just enjoy the bonus!"

"The bonus is not what I want!" Raquel surprised herself again as she found herself standing up at Nordstrom's desk. She put a hand to her belly, working to control the panic. She wasn't used to this kind of confrontation.

All at once, she felt the desperate need to get out of Nordstrom's office. She needed to be somewhere, anywhere else. Raquel backed away from the desk, her breathing getting faster. She felt the same rush at the back of her head that she had when she collapsed in the grocery store, and her stomach twisted with worry as she considered having another panic attack right here, right now.

"Responsibility can't really be what you want," Nordstrom reached a spotted hand across the table in her direction. "Just think it over."

"I'm sorry," Raquel muttered. "I think I need to go."

She tripped as she stepped backward toward his office door and fell flat on her bum. Nordstrom heaved himself up from behind his desk and ambled over to her, puzzling her out with that infuriating sympathy still hanging on his face. The cat on his poster was positioned just behind his head. Animal and man wore the same stupid expression, one that both baffled and incensed Raquel.

"There's no need to have a conniption," Nordstrom lectured her. "You just need to hang in—"

"Don't say it!" Raquel winced. She couldn't take any more pity. "Just... just shut up!"

She scrambled to her feet and darted out the doorway.

Raquel's heart was really racing now. It felt like it might beat right out of her chest. She had never spoken to a boss that way. She had never spoken to *anyone* that way.

But she had been pushed past her breaking point. Her ex's engagement, her boss turning her down for a promotion, her panic attack in the middle of Vons... they were all symptoms. Signs that something needed to change.

And she had to be the one to buck up and change them.

Raquel paused outside of Nordstrom's office, her whole body hesitating as she came to a decision. Confrontation was against her nature. Asking for what she wanted was against her nature. But something had to change. Something had to give. Taking a deep breath, Raquel grabbed the handle and let herself back in.

"I quit," she announced, having to squeeze her eyes shut as she said the words.

Nordstrom looked up from his desk, blinking too much as though he had already forgotten who she was.

"I can stick around for the customary two weeks, but then I'm gone."

The corners of her boss's mouth twitched. He cocked his head, looking even more like the odd, ugly poster cat than before. "Come on, Rachel," he started. "This is an overreaction. You said yourself that we're short-staffed and seeing more patients lately. We need you more than ever."

"Don't worry," she assured him. "I'm sure you'll *hang in there.*"

She hopped back through the door, shutting it behind her. She flew through the hospital hallways until she was outside, feeling the hot, Vegas air ballooning up in her lungs.

Raquel fished around in her purse until she found her cell phone. She dialed her mother. Miriam picked up on the first ring.

"Mama?" Raquel asked. "Can you pull up that email again? I need the contact information."

THREE

TWO WEEKS LATER

WHEN SHE WOKE up two hours into her bus ride, Raquel thought she had made it to Goldfinch, Arizona. The glittering lights of the Vegas strip had long since faded into the background behind her. The air was dustier here, somehow thicker and darker.

But the bus kept driving.

Three hours in and the world had, for the briefest time, turned a shade of green she wasn't accustomed to. Towering trees rose up around her. The air dropped one iota colder. Flat Nevada earth was all but forgotten as foothills rose up from nothingness.

But the bus kept driving.

And then, almost four hours from the time she left her home, her family, and all memories of her life with Jude behind her, the Greyhound stopped. Raquel sat up in her bus seat, pressing the tips of her fingers against the dirty glass.

There was... nothing.

The Vegas lights were gone. The green trees and mountains were gone. What was left was expansive, flat earth. A horizon that faded off into a blurred line where tall, dry grasses met blistering, yellow sun. Her old life, too, was gone.

Raquel followed the few straggling passengers off the bus. She had two bags with her, packed with the bare essentials. In her pockets, she kept only her bus ticket and her cell phone. She felt its weight now, along with a sense of rising panic: was it too early to ring her mother and call this whole thing off?

Come on, chica. Get it together. Raquel straightened her back and stepped off the bus stairs onto the dusty pavement.

Okay. Up closer, the sparse buildings of downtown Goldfinch didn't feel too foreign to her home in Vegas. The Western sun beat down on a bookstore's marquis and sent rainbows shooting down on the pavement. Those were practically casino lights. A lonely gas station on the corner bore a weathered advertisement for scratch-offs and gambling in the window. It was basically the Strip, right?

And just ahead was her destination. Ida's, a little brunch spot painted in quaint yellows and creams, was tucked away at the edge of Main Street. The smell of hickory-smoked bacon and fresh, salted eggs wafted on the breeze. Raquel's stomach complained loud enough for the other bus passengers to hear; she hadn't had the chance to eat any breakfast before getting on the bus. She heaved her two bags into better position on her shoulders and started off.

Raquel paused when she got to the door, rehearsing the millions of possible scenarios in her head. What if her new patient didn't like her? What if she'd left her home and taken a bus ride to the middle of nowhere for *nothing*?

Oh Lord, she'd have to have an actual conversation with a stranger. Someone who would make snap judgements about her rumpled travel clothes or ask her direct questions about why she'd been so eager to skip town. Maybe she should just—

No. Raquel swallowed, thinking back to how she'd quit her job at the hospital, how she'd taken her future into her own hands. She could do this.

The door tinkled like bell chimes when she opened it.

"Sit anywhere, love!"

Raquel followed instructions from a nearby waitress and looked around the restaurant for a window booth. She found one and slid in, nestling her bags on the ground by her feet.

Ida's was cleaner than she had anticipated for a town like Goldfinch. The booths and tables had been kept up with meticulous care, the floors swept and polished to shine. Raquel strained her neck to peer into the little kitchen. Two cooks wore hairnets and gloves as they slaved away over what appeared to be fresh, marbled meats and vegetables. All very reassuring.

Abby would have loved this place.

As soon as Raquel formed the thought, she cringed. It was true though, wasn't it? Ever since they met back in middle school, Abby Hanover had been the kind of girl who was always looking for the local flavor, the little gems that were overlooked by the mainstream. She avoided the Strip, eating at hole-in-the-wall joints in Henderson or Enterprise. When all their friends were buying Nirvana and Radiohead albums, Abby had been exploring up-and-coming pop rock.

It was something Raquel had always loved about her best friend. Though Raquel struggled to form her own identity, Abby always knew who she was. She always did what she pleased. She took what she wanted.

The last thought made Raquel's stomach sour. She did her best to push her ex-best friend from her mind. It was undeniable and unavoidable though; Abby definitely would have loved a quaint little place like Ida's.

"We don't serve mimosas, love, but we do serve a mean Bloody Mary. You'll take that with one of my famous cinnamon rolls?"

Raquel startled at the sound of her waitress at the table. She turned to find a large, round woman watching her, her pen and pad for orders tucked unused under her armpit. The nametag on her heaving bosom read "Ida."

"I... well, yeah," Raquel answered, stammering a bit. "That all sounds really great. How did you—"

"Chef's superpower." Ida tapped the side of her long, pointed nose and winked. "It doesn't hurt that you're the first stranger we've had in town in at least half a year. Which makes you Raquel Villanueva, Adam Gardner's new live-in caretaker."

Raquel had to suppress a giggle at the way Ida pronounced the L's in Villanueva. They must not get a lot of Venezuelan American girls here. It was endearing.

"Jeez, this really must be a small town," Raquel commented, her eyes going wide.

"And the gossip pool is even smaller." Ida surprised her by sliding into the booth across from her and sticking out her hand to shake. "Ida Thomas, the best friend you'll ever make in Goldfinch and the source of your best meal, too. City girls always want a drink with their brunch. And as for the cinnamon roll, well. Turning down a free pastry from me would be a good indicator as to whether or not you were the type of girl who could make it here. You chose wisely, love."

"...*Free* cinnamon roll?" Raquel's stomach rumbled again, somehow even louder than the first time.

Ida shrugged. "Of course," she winked again. "We

Goldfinch folks like a woman with a little meat on her bones."

Raquel's sense of decorum insisted that she hold out until Ida was gone to eat the cinnamon roll, but she couldn't wait any longer. She picked up her fork and tore in, wolfing down most of the pastry in less than a handful of bites.

Ida's eyebrows went up. "Yes'm, I don't think you'll have a problem fitting in here at all."

Raquel blushed and tried to force herself to slow down. "I forgot to eat breakfast before I left home, and now I'm ravenous." She dabbed at her mouth with a napkin. "I'm supposed to be meeting Adam here to get started right now. Has he—do you know—well, would you happen to know if he's around?"

Ida laughed. The sound of it only made Raquel like her more; Ida's laugh was rich and booming, like it came from deep within the wells of her chest, simmering happily below until it was ready to boil over. "Love, I know everyone in this town."

She slid back out of the booth and waved over across the restaurant. Ida put a hand on Raquel's table. "He's not here, but don't fret. Wait a moment, and we'll get ya sorted out," she smiled. "You'll come back now, ya hear?"

"Yes, ma'am," Raquel found herself agreeing. And she meant it.

"Oh!" Raquel added hastily, waving to Ida. "Do you have a phone here?"

Ida nodded. "There's one in the back for take-out orders."

"Would you mind if I give my family your number?" Raquel asked. "I can already tell that my cell phone service is spotty here, and I want to be sure they can reach me."

"Sounds like a good way to get you back here giving me

more Gardner family gossip." Ida smiled and snorted at her own joke as she headed over to her waiting customers.

Between the great brunch place, the welcoming committee, and the free food, Goldfinch was turning out to be a pleasant surprise. Sure, it wasn't the comfortable home in Vegas that Raquel had known for all her life. But maybe she could make it work here. Maybe her mother had been right: a change of pace and environment could be good for Raquel. She could get lost in that dreamy, Western fairytale sunrise, maybe even find herself a handsome rancher. She could forget all about Jude and the—. She stopped herself. She'd almost said the W-word. *Engagements ended all the time.*

She was jerked back to reality when another stranger slid into the booth across from her. Someone who was— once again—decidedly not her new patient Adam Gardner.

"Raquel! It is so wonderful to meet you in person."

The girl sitting across from her had white-blonde hair, enormous blue eyes, and a wide smile that threatened to burst right off of her face. She extended a hand over the remnants of the cinnamon roll.

Raquel took the stranger's hand and shook it, hesitant. "Um, hi?"

The girl shook her head. "Oh Lord, I'm so sorry. I didn't properly introduce myself. I'm Mary Gardner, Adam's younger sister. I've been handling his help-wanted ad and coordinating your arrival."

"Oh, wonderful!" Raquel smiled. She glanced around the restaurant. "Is he—"

"He's back at the house." Mary's voice was clipped. She took Raquel's hand in her own and squeezed. "His place is just off my parents' property. We'll meet him soon. In the meantime, how's about I give you an overview of your day to day before you meet him?"

"Definitely, of course." Raquel pushed aside her breakfast and folded her hands in front of her. "I'm sure you're already aware that I'm qualified to carry out any doctor-ordered treatments Adam might need. As a registered nurse, I have plenty of experience maintaining medical equipment, taking care of sanitary needs—"

Mary waved her off. "You'll find we're a little more low-key than all that. Adam was injured several years ago and he hurt his leg real bad. Walks with a cane most of the time now. It was a mess, lots of hospital visits and even a kidney transplant. Nasty business."

Raquel's eyes widened. A transplant patient wasn't quite as "low-key" as Mary was insisting. "I'm sorry, a transplant patient?" She repeated. "Do you think you could tell me a little more about that—"

But the Gardner sister plowed on in her descriptions, clearly used to talking enough to hold up two sides of a conversation. She waved off Raquel. "Well, it was kind of a necessity because of the damage he did from all of his drug use."

Raquel's eyebrows went up. "He has a drug problem, too?"

"Well not, *anymore*. It was pain management, ya know? He didn't handle it well. Anyway, he developed a clotting problem shortly after," Mary continued. "It's been a nightmare, and with some new swelling he's been having lately, his doctor has advised him to start taking it easy. Between the old injury and the newer issues, he has mobility problems and..."

Mary's voice faltered as she searched for the right words.

Raquel sat up, her ears pricking. It was the first time Mary had even stopped for breath.

"And..." Mary tried to continue. "It's left him with other problems as well. Your duties as an actual nurse would be minimal. What Adam needs is more of, say, companionship."

"I'm sorry?" Raquel shook her head.

"He needs a friend," Mary explained. She sighed at the last word, as though she were too tired to try to phrase things with a better euphemism.

The Gardner sister wasn't meeting Raquel's eye. And there it was: the other shoe was dropping. Cute brunch place, welcoming committee, free food...who cared about any of it if it was all a sham to get Raquel to walk away from the job she'd been working at for years to take care of some almost-thirty-year-old grown man in need of occasional conversation? Her stomach turned. She placed both hands on the table, screwing up all her nerve to look back up at Mary.

"I'm sorry, Miss Gardner," she apologized, looking uncomfortable. "I came for a nursing job, and I'm not sure that being a patient's 'friend' exactly fits my qualifications. This town is very different than my own, and coming here was already out of my comfort zone. I'm not sure that this is the fit for me—"

"Just give him a shot," Mary insisted. She reached out and took Raquel's wrist. "Come to the house. Meet Adam. It will be worth your while."

"Miss Gardner—"

"I'll buy you another cinnamon roll?" Mary smiled. She waved at Ida, who was helping a couple on the other side of the restaurant. "We can take it to go!"

"I'm sorry," Raquel said. She tried to make her voice

sound firm and commanding. Lately, she was getting more practice at that than she'd like. She gathered her stuff and stood up to leave, face burning from anything remotely resembling confrontation.

But Mary pulled her back toward the table.

"Did you know that my ma had cousins all the way out in Maine who got the ad we emailed around?" Mary cleared her throat. "It got sent around more times than we ever thought possible. But we only got a handful of replies. And all of them were the same. They were from female nurses who were open about looking for a fresh start, a new place to start over. Everyone but you told the same story. So the way I figure, you must have the same motivations in taking this post. 'Cept the thing you're running away from is bad enough that you don't want to tell some stranger all the details. You need this job, Raquel. And we would very much like for you to take it."

Raquel was flabbergasted. She put a hand on her hip and cocked her head at Mary. "Ok, seriously, what is it with you small-town folks predicting every part about me? Ida even guessed my breakfast order."

Mary smiled and slid out of the booth. "Well, that's Ida's superpower." She explained. "As for my intel, Goldfinch is a small town but—"

"The gossip pool is smaller?" Raquel supplied.

Mary nodded. "We don't have much to discuss except for pretty new strangers coming to town." She gestured toward the door of the restaurant before scooping up one of Raquel's bags from the floor. "Come on. I'll give you a ride over to Adam's place. Just check it out. That can't hurt, right?"

Raquel paused for a minute thinking, and then nodded. She had another choice, and she knew it. She could walk away now, go back to the life she knew in Vegas. The discomfort she would experience there. The painful memories. Or she could press forward and take the first steps in taking charge of her own life for once.

Sure, there was something off about Adam Gardner. Considering how much his sister was fumbling over discussing him, that was clear enough. But he couldn't be *that* bad.

Could he?

FOUR

"SHOOT ME, NUMSKULL! I DARE YOU!"

Raquel clutched at the porch railing of Adam Gardner's home while Mary Gardner pounded on his door.

"Cowboy up, Adam!" Mary called. "You need a nurse, and I found you one!"

"So help me, Mare, I never asked you to do that!" The voice that came from behind the thin, wooden door was deeper than Raquel had expected.

When Mary told her about Adam's medical history, Raquel had pictured someone wan and frail. Her uncle, Eduardo, had died before he could get a heart transplant. When she'd gone to his funeral, Raquel had thought he looked more alive dead than he did hanging out in the hospital. She'd expected her patient to be like *that*. Certainly not to have the voice of George Clooney. Once again, she was reminded that this job might not be quite what she'd read about in the ad.

She mustered up her courage and tapped Mary at the shoulder. Adam's sister stopped mid-pound to whip around to her, still furious from her encounter with her brother.

"I'm sorry," Raquel started. "I didn't realize you put the ad out without Adam's permission. Clearly, Mr. Gardner can take care of himself, and he certainly doesn't *sound* too broken and sick—"

"Listen to Nurse Ratched out there!" The voice from behind the door was emphatic.

"Hey!" Raquel started. She didn't have much time to feel offended though. Mary cut her off, pounding the door again.

"Adam Samuel Gardner, you will let this girl in and let her take care of you! I will not have Sue Enfield and Lilly Bennett gossiping about how the Gardner family is host to Goldfinch's own Boo Radley."

"Don't make me call Officer Callahan," Adam shot back. "He'll never let you date his son if he has a memory of putting you in handcuffs."

Mary balked at that one. "Darn if he ain't right," she admitted under her breath to Raquel. "Bo Callahan is one of the best-looking bachelors in the county. I can't mess that up."

Mary stepped back, crossing her arms and huffing. After a moment of thinking, a solution came to her.

"Alright," she called through the door. "I'll send her packing. But you should know that the minute this girl crosses city lines, I'm calling the hospital. They gave you clear instructions to hire an in-home nurse. I have it on good authority that they can force you into care. You wanna pay a visit to the ward in St. Raphael's?"

There was a long moment of silence as Mary tapped her foot and watched the door handle. Raquel felt her breath catch in her throat.

Every cell of her being screamed to run away from the dispute. It was ingrained in her from a lifetime of habit. Run back to what you know, run away from what has the potential to be scary. Here was a perfect excuse to bow out of a major life change.

But something kept her frozen on that porch. Maybe it was the sheer force of will that was Mary Gardner. Maybe it was just that she didn't have the cash on hand to pay for another bus ticket. But she suspected that, more than anything, it was the voice that came from behind the front door.

There was more to the story there. Raquel decided right then and there that she wanted to know what it was.

The door cracked open. It was dark in the little house, and Raquel couldn't see past a few feet.

"Alright," the voice came again, sounding reluctant. "You can come in."

Mary pushed the door open, and the white-hot Arizona sun spilled through the doorway. He was standing there, his own arms crossed, a sour look on his face as he took her in. Nevertheless, Adam Gardner nodded his head in the standard fashion, and Raquel couldn't help but think that if he had been wearing a cowboy hat, he would be forced to tip it.

"Howdy, ma'am," he started. He sized her up through slanted eyes. "What I'm sure my ever-helpful sister failed to inform you of is my full story. I'm a transplant survivor—"

"Told her that." Mary interjected with a roll of her eyes.

"I'm a high risk for deep vein thrombosis. Which is a blood clotting problem, by the way, in case nursing school didn't prepare you for that—"

"Covered that, too." Mary stuck her tongue out.

"—*And* I'm a recovering drug addict." Adam paused for effect, as though he had this spiel well-rehearsed. "Turns out that pushing all those pain meds on a teenager has a lasting effect. I started with oxy. Turned to heroine. Should I show you the track mark scars on my arm?"

Mary stepped in, lips pursed. "Stop trying to scare her, Adam. She's a nurse. I'm sure she's seen worse than some cowboy in recovery."

Both brother and sister turned to Raquel then; it was clearly her line next.

Raquel balked. Whatever she was supposed to say, the right words weren't coming to her. She gulped deep: she *could not* allow more panic to overtake her. Not when she'd gotten this far.

"Well?" Adam's mouth turned into a frown, and his brow furrowed as he cocked his head at Raquel. "Do you want to come in and start judging me already, or would you rather just sweat it out on my porch?"

"Ugh, try to be nice, neanderthal," Mary rolled her eyes and pushed her way past him. "You can start by judging his personality. He says he uses humor to cope, or something like that."

"I, um..." Raquel was having trouble finding where her voice went. Adam had stepped fully into the light.

The man standing in the doorway perhaps looked even healthier than he sounded. Adam leaned on a cane, a wooden staff that looked hand-carved. Aside from this, though, he looked strong. He was blonde and fair-skinned, built like a Norse god with broad shoulders and long limbs. The cane came off more like his scepter than his medical device. Raquel's new patient might even be—she gulped —*attractive.*

"Did you hire a mute?" Adam turned to his sister, who was helping herself to his pantry. "Is this supposed to challenge my intellect while she heals my body?"

"I'm not mute," Raquel volunteered weakly. Any captivation that she felt was fading as she was reminded of his biting sarcasm. She stepped inside of the house. "I'm Raquel Villanueva. I'm—"

He held up a hand to cut her off and turned back to his sister, skeptical. "Raquel Villanueva," Adam tried the name out in his mouth, rolling its sounds around on his tongue like he was unsure of its taste. "I'm not sure you'll last long enough here for me to memorize all those syllables."

"I'm more than qualified," she assured him. "I can—"

"I've heard it all, ma'am," he assured her, starting to shut the door once more. "Now why don't you hop a bus back home? I can manage without you."

Raquel found herself digging the toe of her shoe into the cracked wood of the front porch, her frustration building up in every tiny muscle. She was getting awful tired of being cut off when she was trying to work up her courage.

"It's just that your sister thinks—"

"Oh, my sister *thinks* enough for the whole town of Goldfinch." Adam smirked. "Thanks, but no thanks, Miss Villenueva, I'm—"

"Rude?" She supplied. Raquel took herself off guard. Adam's eyebrows shot up.

"What a first impression," he mused. "Didn't anyone ever tell you that those count?"

"Don't worry," she assured him, setting her bags on his floor at her feet. "I'm not sure I'll stick around here babying you long enough for that to matter."

Mary cackled as she slapped together a sandwich. Adam turned to his sister, his pale face flushing pink.

"Oh, come on!" Mary laughed. "Just admit she was a good hire."

Raquel felt her own cheeks turning red. This wasn't like her. She wasn't this person, with the snappy comebacks and the witty banter. She had other good qualities, sure, but they weren't these. In fact—she remembered with a sinking feeling in her stomach that she willed back as soon as it came on—that was one of the reasons that Jude had left. She wasn't a challenge. She wasn't confident.

How the heck did a bitter, unlikeable person like her new employer bring it out in her?

But as she listened to Mary laugh and watched Adam's neck darken, Raquel was surprised to find that she might just like this new version of herself. Maybe Goldfinch wasn't what she had thought it was going to be. But maybe it was a chance to start over and reinvent herself. Maybe here she could be snappy, witty Raquel. If Adam Gardner was never going to like her or make her job easy, he could be the perfect target to try her new self out on.

"And who, pray tell, is going to pay for Miss Villanueva here?" Adam asked, looking more than a little surly as he crossed his arms and turned to his sister.

"You are." Mary shrugged, nonchalant.

"I am?" Adam repeated, scoffing.

"Adam, you have all the money in the world from all those years you spent training Buck Johnson's new fillies," Mary explained, holding bold eye contact with her brother. "And in that time, all I've ever seen you purchase for yourself is a new Stetson and sugar snacks from the Stop and Shop. And what's more, it's per doctor's recommendation. Dr. Weller is gonna have a conniption if you show up to your next appointment having forgotten a weekend's worth of meds and reinjured your leg. You can afford this."

"So glad you assessed my finances for me." Adam grunted.

"You're very welcome." Mary crossed her arms and smirked.

Raquel straightened her shoulders and stepped forward, feeling a bit uncomfortable as the Gardner siblings squared off with one another. "Um, I think maybe I'd like a tour now?"

"She'd like a tour." Mary grinned over at her brother, waving them forward.

Adam sized Raquel up once more, examining her from head to toe. She suddenly felt very out of place in her favorite yoga pants and tee, but she kept her back straight and chin forward. She wouldn't let someone like Adam scare her off.

At long last, her new patient sighed and shrugged. "Alright, follow at your own risk."

Raquel trailed Adam down a hallway just off the living room. He kept his space dark; the curtains were drawn over every window and the only light on was the one Mary had flipped on back in the kitchen. It was disorganized and dusty—a true bachelor pad.

"I can feel your judging gaze on the back of my neck, Ratched," Adam commented without turning around. "Keep in mind, this is my parent's mother-in-law suite that I'm renting out. I inherited it this way. Their ranch is just past the trees."

Raquel swallowed. *Keep channeling that confidence. This is your chance to be someone new.* "Yeah, about that Ratched nickname. If we're going to pick a nurse name for me, I think I'd prefer Florence Nightingale or Clara Barton."

Seriously, where was she pulling this stuff from?

Adam snorted as he pressed on with his tour. "Only bathroom is to the left. Spare room is to the right, so I guess that's you. Hope you don't mind cat hair. My grandmother lived here before me, and that's where her three calicos slept."

He turned back, gauging her reaction. He was testing her, probing for a way to get her out of his house.

"I love cats," Raquel insisted. "You can try to get rid of me again later, Mr. Gardner."

Adam stopped in the hall and turned to her. She was following too close and almost bumped right into his chest. She gulped; this close to him, Raquel realized just how big Adam really was. It wasn't just that his shoulders were broad or his limbs long; he was built like a tank. She had to tilt her chin just to look up at him. Nevertheless, she held his gaze, assembling every last ounce of courage she had.

"Remember, I'm a recovering drug abuser," he said, his voice blunt. "Sometimes I still have night terrors about the withdrawal. I'm told I can scream in my sleep."

"I sleep with a sound machine." Raquel shrugged. She'd dealt with burnouts before at the hospital. *You can do this.*

"My parents visit. Often." He continued, still staring her dead in the eye. "So do my siblings, of which I have six. No privacy here."

"I'm an only child," Raquel replied. Her typically small voice was evening out, relinquishing its standard quiver. "Always wanted the big family experience."

"My leg is my primary injury," he said. "It swells and gives me a lot of pain. Whatever will you do if I fall in the bathroom and can't get up?"

She took a deep breath and offered up the best snarky smile she could. "Well, if you keep up this attitude, maybe I'll just let you die half-naked by the toilet and tell your family I couldn't get to you in time?"

Mary stepped between them, still cackling at their exchange. "You're so hired it's not even funny," she informed Raquel. "I'll get you a check every two weeks." She turned back to her brother. "Don't you *dare* scare her off."

Mary slipped back down the hallway, waving behind her. "Also, you're out of smoked gouda!"

Adam's face soured further, but he stayed looking at his new nurse. "You can take the rest of the night off," he said after a pause. Maybe he was growing tired of thinking up insults. "I have a follow-up appointment tomorrow morning for a surgery I had last month. You capable of driving me there?"

"Um, yes, sure, more than capable," she replied, nodding. Ah, there was the stammering. Free of the tight banter she'd been exchanging with her new employer, Raquel found herself fumbling back to the safety of shy, unsure responses. She had swallowed hard and forced herself not to look down at her feet.

"Alright then," Adam's voice was begrudging, but she did notice a flicker in his blue irises. This wouldn't be the end of his interrogation; Raquel was sure of that. "I'm off to take a nap. You can feed yourself from my kitchen, Florence. Lord knows my sister already did."

She nodded again as he walked off to his bedroom. She could see the slight limp to his gait now, the pain that was clearly evident with each step.

Raquel let herself into her new room. She sat down on the bed; things looked even more bleak in the bedroom than they had out in Adam's crowded family room. The room was cramped and tiny. Faded, half-stripped wallpaper adorned the walls, patterned to look like various flora and fauna. The details of the room were all antique: the light fixture above Raquel's head was a dusty bowl attached to an aging fan, framed pictures of a farmer couple had been printed in black and white, and the air smelt like ancient, crumbling potpourri. It was a far cry from what she would have expected a bachelor pad to look like. Worse, it was a far cry from her familiar home back in Vegas.

But despite the grim surroundings, Raquel smiled as she sat down on her new bed.

Adam Gardner was going to be a challenge in more ways than one. He might not be as ill as she once thought, but he had enough bite to him that Raquel would be kept on her toes. Her smile grew bigger as she thought back to how he'd called her Florence instead of Ratched before he left for his nap. Maybe there was some hope for him after all.

Once again, she found herself itching to pick up her cell phone and make a call. She could almost hear Abby's voice on the end of the line. How she'd say "Yello?" like it was the funniest pun in the world.

But as soon as Raquel replayed the exchange in her mind, she felt the smile fade from her lips. She could hear just as clearly the last conversation she'd had with Abby. She could still feel the sting of betrayal, the disappointment rumbling in the pit of her stomach.

Going from "Ratched" to "Florence" over the course of one conversation was a sign of great promise for her employment with Adam Gardner. She could make this work.

After all, she had to.

FIVE

WHATEVER CONFIDENCE RAQUEL had felt upon meeting her new patient was quickly dissipating.

The night before, she had fallen asleep face first on the bed in her tiny, darkened bedroom. She hadn't even bothered to take off her makeup. Instead, she'd given into the crushing weight of all her anxieties: a new job, a new town, and a new employer who decidedly did not want her around. It had all been too much. Raquel had spent the entire afternoon holed up in her bed with the curtains drawn tight, eyes squeezed shut as she weighed out the merits of sticking it out in Goldfinch or returning home.

At some point, she must have fallen asleep, although she couldn't have said when. Adam had been up bright and early, knocking on the door of her bedroom by six a.m. for her to get dressed so they could hit the road. They'd loaded into his old, weathered truck—Raquel still wearing day-old contacts and trying to rub out the imprint of patchwork quilt on her right cheek—and they headed off for his doctor's appointment in Prescott. Her stomach was rumbling loudly as it had the morning before. It was hard to ignore it as they drove by Ida's restaurant on the way out of town.

In an effort to distract herself and reiterate the potential merits of her new job, Raquel asked Adam questions about their visit. She'd inquired about his family and his interests and whatever else she could think of to fill the silence. In return, Adam had supplied her with one-word answers as he stared out the window of the passenger seat. His shoulders were hunched away from her, his whole body warning her to back off. Twenty minutes had never felt more like four hours.

He wasn't doing much to help the case for her sticking around at this new job.

The parking lot was empty when they pulled in, but Adam hopped out and headed right for the doors.

"Are they even open?" Raquel called after him.

"They are for me, Florence," he assured her. Sure enough, he'd pulled open the glass doors to the office and the receptionist waved him and Raquel back without their even signing in.

Adam took a sharp left down a dark hallway, taking the liberty of flipping the light switch as he passed it. The cane he carried with him clacked at a brisk, practiced pace and Raquel struggled to keep up, her short legs having to work double time as he strode toward room number five and let himself in.

Raquel was learning more from Adam's silent actions than she believed she would have from any conversation they might have had in the car. His movements were methodical, but impatient. He'd been here before. Many times. Probably too many; he knew every turn and worked the building in a way that Raquel had never seen from a patient before. He moved fast, too, like he was eager to get it over with. But there was a sharpness to his movements, maybe a bit of a shake to his fingers as he opened doors and switched on lights.

It struck her then: he was nervous.

Despite all of her hesitancies, she could feel the old nursing instincts kicking in. She took a seat in a chair next to Adam in the little room and put a hand on his arm. "These visits never get easier, huh?"

His response was more annoyed than expected. "I'm not scared," he snapped. "I just move fast. I need Dr. Weller to get in here before—"

The door opened then, and Adam groaned and slid down in his chair.

"You didn't wake us up?" A woman, as blonde and fair as Adam but quite a bit older, slipped into the room. With one decisive flick of her wrist, she motioned for him to let her have his chair and for him to take the medical bench instead. "I had to throw on my gardening clothes when I heard your truck leaving the house. I am *mortified*, Adam. I can't believe Dr. Weller is going to see me this way, we've been going to him for *years*—"

"Florence, this is my mother. Esther." Adam gestured, looking even more annoyed than when they had entered the waiting room.

Esther turned to Raquel with a look of surprise on her face, as though she had only just realized she wasn't alone with her son. "Oh, Lord!" Her hand flew to her chest before she extended it for shaking. "The new nurse! It's lovely to meet you, Florence. We've been trying to get Adam to hire someone for forever. You are an angel on earth."

"Um, my name's Raquel, actually," she corrected, her cheeks flushing despite her best efforts.

Esther glanced, puzzled, over to Adam. His face split into a sly grin. "Wait, your name's not Florence?" she asked. Adam laughed.

The door swung open again. Everyone in the little room looked up as Mary entered, followed by a tall, thin redhead. Adam's groan was the loudest one yet.

"What is this, a family reunion?" he bemoaned.

"I'm so sorry that we care about you," the ginger scolded him, a half-smile threatening to overtake her lips. "But you had to know I was coming. I've got Angela back at the house watching Elliott for the morning, and Jack made tentative plans to reschedule the meeting with Hank Buller if you needed us to bring you anything from town. Consider yourself lucky he's not here, too, you know how Jack gets about your health updates—"

Raquel shifted in her seat, and the metal squealed on the tile floor. The redheaded girl looked over to her, eyes wide as though she had only just realized that the family wasn't alone.

She extended a hand out to Raquel. "I'm Grace, Adam's oldest sister. Are you the nurse that responded to our ad?"

Raquel nodded. She felt a heat rising up from her collar; all of these people in such a small room was starting to get to her. "Yes, I'm—"

The door swung open yet again, but this time a middle-aged doctor slid through the small gap between sisters to get to the center of the room.

"Dr. Weller, you are a sight for sore eyes." Adam perked up from his spot on the bench. "I need medical attention right away, or I might be subject to injury in such an over-crowded room."

Dr. Weller winced, but smiled. "I'm sorry, Adam. We have a new nurse in the back, and the girls were on your HIPAA forms. They got the appointment reminder call when you didn't pick up."

"And now you'll have our moral support, whether you like it or not." Mary grinned. "Lay it on us, doc. We want the news."

For the first time since Esther's arrival, the room went quiet. Dr. Weller shuffled papers around on his clipboard.

Raquel felt her stomach take a dip. She knew this pause. It wasn't good. She stole a glance over at Adam, knowing that if she stayed quiet enough, none of the Gardner family would remember the lackluster nurse tucked away into the corner behind Grace and Mary.

Yet again, she found herself surprised by Adam. The signs were all laid out that this appointment was a big deal. He'd hired a live-in nurse beforehand; his sisters and mother had felt compelled to come along. But it wasn't the expected fear that she saw on Adam's face. It was something else, something suspended between anxiety and self-loathing that was dangerously close to embarrassment. In fact, it was a look that she was sure she wore herself on a regular basis.

He wasn't scared. It seemed clear that Adam had had this conversation a million times before, with a million doctors before this one. Instead, he was miserable, ashamed. There was something buried just beneath his eyes that hinted at a pain deeper than the one in his leg. Adam had been through it. Raquel knew it, and it was more than her experience as a nurse that was telling her that.

"We need to get you back for a quick little procedure today," Dr. Weller explained, tucking the clipboard under his arm.

"Another operation?" Esther's eyes went wide.

"Today?" Grace's expression mirrored her mother's.

"What is it?" Mary asked. "How can we help?"

"It's just a simple placement for an IVC filter," Dr. Weller assured them. Adam's family stared back at him blankly, and Raquel assumed that this was a term with which they weren't familiar. Dr. Weller cleared his throat to continue. "It's a tiny device we place in Adam's chest to prevent blood clots."

"Isn't that what he takes blood thinners for?" Mary asked.

"Besides, wouldn't the clots be in his leg?" Grace chimed in.

"Yes and yes," Dr. Weller confirmed. "I'm troubled by some of the leg swelling that Adam described at his last visit. As I've told you before, his accident all those years ago injured a deep vein, and between that and his family history of blood clots, I think we need to stay on top of this. It's a minimally invasive procedure, with a great track record. At worst, Adam will get some dull, aching pain after. Normally it could take a day or two for scheduling, but I guess this a perk of being a small town with few patients like Adam, huh?"

Dr. Weller smiled at the girls like he was telling a funny joke. None of them responded, so he turned back to his paperwork once more, clearing his throat. "We'll get Adam back now to sign off on the paperwork and get the full explanation, set him up with some pain meds, and get him back home."

"What about his blood thinners?" Esther asked. "Will he still need those, too?"

"I'd like to keep him on them in addition to the IVC

filter," Dr. Weller agreed. "With his family history and his previous transplant, we're never really going to be out of the woods when it comes to deep vein thrombosis. He needs to keep taking those blood thinners, no matter what."

With no warning, Adam lurched up from his spot on the bench and grabbed for his cane. "I'm sure if I made it in here today, then we can put this off a little longer, right? Come up with some alternative therapies—"

"Sit back down!" The Gardner girls all snapped in unison. Raquel's eyes were tired from darting back and forth between the family members.

Adam stiffened before he took his seat.

"I can stay over with him tonight," Grace volunteered. "Jack can watch Elliott by himself. They'll be fine."

"That's what we hired Raquel for, remember?" Mary reminded her.

"I'm still here, you know," Adam reminded his sisters. His voice was sharp. Irritated.

"At the very least, we can take turns bringing food," Esther commented. "I've got a casserole in the freezer."

"All he's got is basic sandwich stuff," Mary said. "I was just there yesterday."

"I can take care of myself," Adam jumped in. He shifted in his seat. His arms were tense; his knuckles were white where they gripped his chair. None of his family members seemed to take notice.

"We'll need to make a grocery run."

"Five o'clock okay for you both?"

"Dr. Weller, will he be out by five?"

"*I'm the patient, damn it!*" Adam stood up then. He staggered a little with the effort, his balance clearly having been thrown onto his weak leg. On instinct, Raquel's arm shot out to offer help. He rejected it, instead crossing his arms as his sisters and mother turned to him, eyebrows raised, as though they had all but forgotten he was even there with them.

There—Raquel saw it again. A flash in the deep blue of his eyes. Adam wanted out of that room. He wanted out *now*.

They were the same, she and Adam. She knew it then. Both were powerless to have a little control in their lives. Maybe it wasn't fair of Raquel to compare her inability to keep a boyfriend committed to Adam's health plight, but as a nurse she was trained to find common ground where she could. And this was definitely that.

Her heart ached for him. He needed an out, even if his well-meaning family didn't want to give him one.

Before she knew what she was doing, Raquel stood up and passed him his cane. "Do you need a little privacy to think about this, Adam? Dr. Weller could go over the procedure with you alone?"

Grace shot out of her chair and put an arm up to stop them from heading to the doorway. "Come on, we've been in this together for years. There's nothing we haven't heard before."

Raquel put her own hand out, touching it to Grace's forearm, gentle, but firm. Grace's eyes flared, and Raquel pulled her hand back almost as quick as she'd put it there. She gulped. She felt the now familiar wave of sweat. Numbness. Nausea. She fought against the panic rising in her chest.

"I'm not saying he needs you cut out of his life completely," she explained slowly. "But in my experience, some patients prefer a little privacy to go over all their options. And I am the nurse you hired, after all."

Her heart was thumping so hard she could feel it

vibrating across her skin. But she stuck out her chin, anyway. *I am the nurse you hired, after all.* If she could say it out loud, she could force herself to believe in her own confidence.

Out of the corner of her eye, Raquel could see Adam glancing down at her, one eyebrow raised in surprise. Her heart beat harder.

"Come on," Grace continued. "I just think—"

"I have to insist," Raquel reaffirmed. Headache. Fingers tingling. Heart pounding. She clenched her fists at her side; she *would not* give in to the anxiety.

At last, Grace stepped back, hands in the air. "Alright," she conceded. "But the only conclusion is that he's getting that procedure."

Mary and Esther murmured their agreement, but they stayed seated.

Dr. Weller gestured for their exit to head to another room. "Shall we?"

"We shall," Adam announced. He gestured with his hand for Raquel to head out first. "After you, Commander Nightingale. The only person on earth to ever get three Gardner women to shut up at once."

She knew he was joking. But as they left the room full of his sister and mother to head to another room next door, Raquel couldn't help but think that there was an edge of admiration to his voice, maybe even interest.

As soon as she thought *that* though, she reminded herself not to believe it. Adam was cute. Clearly, he brought out a side of Raquel that had lain dormant before. But she shouldn't imagine interest where there was none. She had believed that Jude had been interested in her once. That he had maybe even loved her. Look how that turned out.

What was even more important was that Adam was both

her employer and her patient. She had a duty here, both professional and ethical. She needed to be very careful not to let herself blur the lines between friendliness and friendship.

Raquel would play Florence for Mr. Gardner. And that was it.

SIX

THE COURAGE RAQUEL had mustered back at the doctor's office to defend Adam's sense of control had dissipated as she drove him back home.

He was sitting in the passenger seat, a tiny bag of pain meds balanced on his lap. He looked at them like they might as well be poison. Adam hadn't wanted them; he hadn't even wanted the procedure. He had finally agreed, but only on the condition that it be up to him whether or not he needed to take the pills. Dr. Weller's team had fixed him up fast, sent him packing to the pharmacy before heading home, and Raquel was left with zero ideas on how to get from Point A to Point B in her new employment relationship.

She thought of a few questions to ask. She came up with some lame conversation starters, but she just knew Adam would go back to calling her Ratched as soon as she whipped those out. They were pulling up to his little house before she ever worked up the nerve to ask him anything at all.

Adam let himself out of the car and limped up to his front door. Raquel turned off the truck and jogged to catch up, but he was locking himself in his room before she had even shut the screen behind her. The little white bag of prescription pills had been dropped at the top of the waste basket.

Raquel sighed and crossed her arms. One step forward with her new patient, two limping steps back.

With Adam gone, she pulled a small pad and pen out of a kitchen drawer. She started to draw up a list of the daily duties she should be performing as an in-home caretaker. Sure, the Gardner clan hadn't exactly been very clear about what they expected from her, but that didn't mean that she was going to slack off. Besides, if Raquel was facing obstacles and anxieties at every turn, a little work-focused distraction could be very good for her.

She jotted down the obvious first: *Administer meds. Review vitals daily. Redress incision site.* She sucked on her pen before adding *Pick up house. Improve handicap accessibility. Provide medical literature.*

Raquel added a few more notes and then set aside the pen and paper. Unfortunately, none of this work really applied until Adam's wound needed redressing, and if she got caught cleaning up his house or attempting to add a ramp over the stairs on his front porch in the light of day, Adam might just shoot her on sight. Better to rest up now and set to work when she knew for sure that he was out for the night.

Besides, if Adam was going to call it a day, she might as well settle in. She headed down the hall in the direction of her new bedroom.

Raquel ducked into her room and shut the door behind her, pressing her back up against the wood as she ran her fingers through her hair. Her bags were still packed, neat and pretty, in the corner of the tiny room.

She walked over, one finger sliding along the bumps of the zipper. It still wasn't too late to go back. Was she cut out for this? Adam was a challenge, to be sure. And his family was another demanding element on top of that. Maybe Raquel had done what she needed to do in helping Adam to put a moment of distance between himself and his family. Maybe that was her grand calling, to help him take back a little control in his life.

Raquel sat down on the edge of her bed and collapsed back onto the quilt. The irony of her "helping" Adam Gardner wasn't lost on her. Running off to Goldfinch, Arizona to aid an injured cowboy was just another way of her avoiding having to take control of her own life.

When she closed her eyes, she could almost see a ticking clock imprinted on the insides of her eyelids: Abby and Jude's wedding was getting closer by the day. There were likely just a few months left for Raquel to get herself back in control, to convince herself that was worth more than one failed relationship. Too bad that her first step in the direction of self-healing had ended with a patient who may very well fire her before morning if his frustrated sisters didn't do it themselves.

But she didn't want to think about that. Raquel buried her face in the down pillow and let loose a muffled scream. She didn't what to do. Just like in the ice cream aisle at Vons, she was paralyzed. Frozen.

IT WAS TOTALLY dark when Raquel woke up. Something was outside her window.

She bolted upright, pulling the quilt up tight around her body on instinct. She hadn't meant to fall asleep like that, on top of the covers. Had anyone thought to check the locks on the doors before bed? Was Adam okay?

Raquel shivered. She strained her foggy brain to remember what kind of animals roamed the deserts of Goldfinch at night. She thought back to a picture of a mountain lion she'd seen in a college textbook. Its eyes had glowed, and its teeth were razor sharp. The shiver raced through her body again.

The sound came once more, a low, agonizing moan.

Raquel forced herself to slide off the edge of the bed and inch toward her window. Was something in pain out there? Maybe she should go check. Her stomach knotted up. She really, *really* didn't want to do that.

"Come on," she whispered to herself, trying to hype up a little nerve. "Girl, you have sedated a juiced-up bouncer with knuckle tattoos. You can do this."

Raquel bounced on the balls of her feet. Finally, a fragile ounce of bravery bubbled up inside of her. She jumped on it, bolting out the doorway, down the hall, and straight through the front door.

"Argh!!" She gestured with wild limbs, sending out a quick prayer that God might let her scare off whatever animal was lurking on the porch.

"Good night, nurse!" Adam Gardner choked on a gulp of water he had just taken. His glass flew out of his hands and exploded on the hard dirt just off to the side of the porch.

Raquel winced. She felt the heat of embarrassment inching up her neck and onto her cheeks. She scrambled over to grab Adam's hands. "I am so sorry," she said. "You didn't get any glass on your fingers, did you? I should have looked before I rushed out like that. I thought you were a—"

She stopped short, holding his fingers in her open palm.

They were shaking, a quiver so small she could barely see it. Adam yanked back his hand, burying it in his pocket.

"I'm fine," he muttered, waving for her to go back to bed. "Just getting a little midnight drink."

But Raquel couldn't just go back to her bedroom. Adam was huddled over under his own patchwork quilt, the fabric wrapped tight around his bulky form. His handsome, thick locks of hair were matted to his temples as a thick sheen of sweat shimmered in the porch light.

"Have you—" Raquel cleared her throat, trying to channel the assertiveness she'd felt at the doctor's office today. "Have you been keeping on top of your pain meds?"

Adam laughed. The sound didn't bear any trace of humor. "Ask the trash can in the kitchen." He braced his hands on the porch railing, hanging his head. "I don't do pain meds."

He rubbed the back of his neck. Raquel saw it again—his hands were shaking. And then it clicked.

"You won't take the meds... because of your addiction." Raquel guessed. She took one cautious step in his direction, feeling more than a little worried she might scare him out of talking to her.

Adam didn't look up. "Dr. Weller knows my history," he said. "He wouldn't prescribe me something if the pain wasn't going to be intense. It's just... I thought I could handle it."

"Why didn't you say that back at the office?" Raquel asked. "You could have talked it through. I'm sure he would understand."

"But would my sisters? Would my mom?" He shot back. Adam looked up at her then, his blue eyes flashing.

"Come on," Raquel started. "There's HIPPA—"

"Yeah," Adam snorted. "Because *HIPPA* did me a lot of good keeping them from my appointment today. I outright cursed at them back there, and they still didn't seem to hear me."

He crossed his arms and walked away from her, shaking his head. He let the quilt slip from his shoulders and fall to the ground as he walked.

Raquel felt the breath catch in her throat, a sensation not too unlike when she'd had her panic attack in the grocery store. Adam had his shirt off. The tanned, thick muscles on his arms were all exposed, glinting in the low light. She forced herself to look down at the ground. Seriously, what kind of nurse checked out their patient when they were at such a low point?

"Adam," she started, refocusing. "Your family loves you. That's more than a lot of my patients could ask for. A support system goes a long way. I'm sure you've heard that at Narcotics Anonymous or something."

"Sure, their support goes a long way, but so does their sympathy." Adam turned back to her, his face contorted with emotion. "Did you see the way they looked at me back there when Dr. Weller told them I needed another procedure? Poor Adam, the Gardner family charity case. If they ever saw me fall back into addiction, I'll just be letting them down all over again. I'll die under the weight of their disappointment."

Raquel took another step toward him, her hand reaching out just an inch closer to his on the railing. "You can't think that way," she told him. "You need these pain meds, and I'm the nurse who can help you control your taking them. Relapse is the absolute worst thing that could happen. It's so far off, you can't allow yourself to think about it."

"It already happened." Adam's voice had gone very small and quiet. He wasn't looking at her now. His eyes were trained on a far-off spot in the darkness, where even the shadows had melded together into blackness. "It was a year ago. Another procedure. I didn't... I didn't go back to the hard stuff. I didn't let it get that far. But it could have. I felt it inside of me, that need to use again. It never disappears. It just waits. It waits until a moment of weakness."

He looked so tired. Adam had borne these feelings for too long. Raquel held her breath as she crossed over to him and placed her hands next to his, almost touching now, on the railing.

"My boyfriend left me for my best friend four months ago." The words were coming out without her deciding to speak them.

Adam looked up at her, one eyebrow raised. "You can't just change the subject to make me feel better."

"I'm not—" Raquel started. She shook her head. "No. That's not what I'm doing. Come on."

Adam crossed his arms as he turned to her.

"He didn't give me any warning," she went on. "Three years together. We had an apartment, a life. And four months later he was proposing to a girl I introduced him to, with a ring I'd been eyeballing in a Vera Wang catalogue. But the worst part wasn't even the breakup, it was the way that Jude looked at me when we spoke in person. The way that *Abby* looked at me. They were both dripping with so much pity—"

"I still think my sob story has you beat," Adam said. "You can't win this contest."

"That's not the point," Raquel shook her head again. "Look, I'm just saying that I get it, okay? I understand the pity looks, the 'helpful' family members, all of it. And more than anything, I understand the lack of control. The sense that your whole world is spinning out from underneath you, and you'll drown in dry air."

"That's exactly it." She could barely hear the words come out of his mouth. It was as though this was only the first time he had given the thought any real life, like the concepts were too terrifying or personal to say out loud. "No one has ever really put it that way before. Like they understand."

"I'm glad I could help," Raquel said. "Even if it's just a little."

"You have," Adam admitted. He cleared his throat. His back straightened the tiniest bit. "I'm sure by now it's clear that I value my independence. I like to solve my own problems. But what you did today, stepping between me and my sisters... it meant a lot."

Adam looked at her again, and this time she could feel it: Raquel remembered what her purpose was in coming to Goldfinch. She and Adam, they needed each other. They needed to help one another recover and move on with their lives and show the world that they had their stuff together. She could do that.

Raquel shivered a bit as a cool evening breeze blew across the porch. She crossed her arms and rubbed her shoulders, thinking.

"We'll try some herbal remedies in the morning," she announced. "I remember a few from my time in school. Oxy is just more popular these days. If those don't work, we can talk mindfulness. Meditation. Maybe even acupuncture if you're feeling crazy."

The corner of Adam's mouth twitched the slightest bit. He picked up the quilt from off the ground and handed it to her. "Stay warm, Florence," he told her. "If you're going to keep me alive, then I need to keep you alive, too."

Raquel took it and wrapped it tight around her body. "Thanks."

She headed back inside. Adam walked around the front of the porch to pick up the jagged pieces of his broken glass, and then followed close behind her.

Raquel felt her own mouth twitch a little. And then, before she knew it, her lips had pulled into a full-blown smile. It felt good to help Adam. Heck, it felt good to help herself.

She stole a glance back at her new patient, hoping that he at least looked a little less depressed even if he still didn't feel the best. He was closing the screen door behind them. His shoulders caught in the light, highlighting his well-toned form.

Raquel's eyes shot back to the path in front of her. *Don't you go fantasizing about your charge.* That wasn't a healthy part of recovery. Not for either of them.

Ethics. Professionalism. Get it together, girl.

SEVEN

SEVEN.

Raquel awoke to the sounds of a rooster crowing. An actual, real-life rooster. The alarm clock read five a.m. It wasn't even light out. She buried her face into her pillow as it screeched just beyond her window.

"Lay off already; I'm up!"

She sat up in her tiny twin bed, having to reorient herself as to where she was. It was two days into her time in Goldfinch. Two days in, and she didn't feel any more comfortable in Adam's home.

"Don't I get a grace period before you start harassing me?" She muttered more to herself than to the rooster. "Two days... haven't even been here long enough to decorate."

Raquel sighed and eyeballed her still-packed bags in the room's one empty corner. She knew that she ought to finally spend a morning unpacking. And last night, after her breakthrough in understanding her new patient, she would have thought that was a great idea. Now, though, the idea of settling into this timeworn room, of trying to make it her own... she didn't exactly relish the prospect.

Raquel swung her legs out of bed and unzipped her duffel just enough to pull out a favorite pair of yoga pants and a sports bra. She switched them out for her pajamas as the rooster started up crowing again.

"I'm leaving, okay? Jeez." She grumbled on her way out the door.

First stop was the hall bathroom, where she'd set down Adam's little baggie of meds the night before. Raquel got herself nice and organized; there was something calming and peaceful about getting back into the groove of regular nursing. Maybe her post was unconventional, but she could lose herself in the predictability of her routine. Raquel prepared his pills in a little paper cup and drew up his blood thinner for injection. She even pulled a little band-aid out of the medicine cabinet for him.

There were sounds of life coming from down the hall. Adam must be awake, typical farm stock. Raquel's chest squeezed tight as she recalled the details of their interaction the night before.

A smile overtook her face at the idea of starting their new regiment together. She needed a new project to dive into. Something she could lose herself in and forget all about the mess she'd left behind back home. She could get Adam started on some essential oils, maybe teach him some stretches that he could do in the morning. It was going to be gr—

Raquel stopped at the entry to the living room.

"Howdy, Florence. You're awake."

Adam was propped up on the couch, a rerun of *Full House* playing on the television. He was dressed in a fluffy robe, his blonde hair a tangled mop on the top of his head. On the couch pillows beside him, junk food wrappers were piled high. And to top it all off, Adam had a metal grabber tool draped across his lap. He picked it up now and used it to wave at Raquel from his spot buried among blankets and cushions.

"Be a doll and make me some coffee? My grabber isn't quite long enough for that." He smirked.

Raquel shook her head to clear it. She set down the tray she'd prepared. "Um..." she started, trying to get her bearings. What happened to the man who had committed to her pain management regiment last night? This guy looked like he had given up on ever even leaving his house.

"How about you get up and I can help you make the coffee yourself?" she suggested. "If pain is a problem, we really ought to work through it together. Working those muscles near where they put in the filter can only help—"

"I think I'm good," Adam said, turning back to the TV to watch Danny Turner vacuuming his stairs. "Besides, I make a crap cup of coffee."

Raquel folded her arms. "Maybe you don't need the coffee at all," she mused. "It looks like you've been up since we talked last night. Maybe instead of caffeine you just need a nap."

"Thanks, Mom." Adam snorted. "If you're not going to make coffee, can you run out to the store for me and buy me a fresh cup? I've got a list going, it's somewhere tacked onto the fridge."

"Adam, come on," Raquel stammered. Her irritation was escalating, and she had to work to control her voice. "Let's go together. We can—"

He gestured with his grabber again. "And hey, if you get a second can you take a look in the bathroom, too? I think there's something wrong with the toilet."

Raquel stomped her foot. "Dang it, Adam Gardner, *I am not your maid.*"

Adam put forth the minimal amount of energy neces-
sary to turn from his spot on the couch cushions, eyebrows
raised.

"Were my sisters not clear that that was part of the job
description?" He asked innocently.

"Oh, they were very clear about my job description,"
Raquel informed him. She crossed over to where he sat and
picked up his remote, turning off *Full House*. Once more, a
brief interaction with her new patient was banishing the
self-doubt and leaving her feeling more than a little
fired up.

"Hey!"

"I'm your nurse, not your mother," she said. "And I
thought we had come to an understanding last night about
how I can help you to overcome these health struggles. You
couldn't get rid of me the first two days I was here, and you
can't get rid of me now."

Adam slouched down further into his spot, rolling his
eyes. "Look, Florence, what do you want from me?" His
voice was quiet. Bitter. "It was all fine and well to talk about
our big plans for a med-free recovery last night, but do you
know what that looks like in reality? It's living off your
couch. Eating takeout because you're too tired and weak to
cook anything. Watching the world go by from a window
because that's all you have left."

Raquel's brow furrowed. "All you have left?" she
repeated. She stuck a hand on her cocked hip. "Adam, you're
in recovery. You're not a total invalid."

He crossed his arms, looking anywhere but up at her.

Raquel spotted a pair of his boots sitting by the door.
She found that little swell of confidence pushing up from
out of her chest, and she seized onto it: she liked this version
of herself so much more than she liked the sniveling,

pathetic mess that she had been lately. She needed to try to lean into this.

Raquel walked over, picked up the boots, and tossed them to him. "That's it," she announced. "No more watching the world go by from a window. Or worse—watching it go by through 90s TV show reruns. We're going outside."

Adam groaned. "This isn't what I'm paying you for."

"Let's be honest, it's your sister coordinating my payments," she reminded him with a smile. "Even if you are the one who's boss. Now get those boots on. We're going for a walk; it's good for recovery."

Adam begrudgingly did as he was told. He got up from the couch and crossed over to where Raquel stood at the front door.

"I'm not changing out of my robe," he announced.

"It's your prerogative," she agreed with a chuckle.

Adam pulled the door open and waved Raquel ahead. They took the stairs together, both looking out to the blue horizon as the faintest hint of orange started to tug at the skyline.

They crossed through the long grasses of his front lawn, walking side by side in silence towards nothing in particular. It was colder outside than Raquel would have guessed. She was regretting her sports bra and yoga pants; she eyed Adam's fluffy white robe with envy.

He had it pulled tight around his chest, the thick material hugging the curves of his arms and shoulders. The cursory glance Raquel had given him sent an unexpected flash of heat rippling across the back of her neck. She crossed her arms and retrained her eyes from the sunrise to the ground beneath her feet.

In what felt like a breath, the world around them went from cool darkness to pink and apricot fire. The sun had finally broken through, shooting out its rays to bathe the world in light. Raquel watched as tiny critters peeked soft, wet noses out from homes in the dirt. Bugs took flight from their places in the grass, buzzing off to some new adventure. The rooster crowed again.

"I can't remember the last time I watched a sunrise."

Adam's voice surprised her. Raquel looked up as they walked. He had his hands in the pockets of his robe as he took in the world's metamorphosis.

"I used to see it every morning when I worked the horses," he continued, his tone hushed and reverent. His eyes crinkled down in the corners. "I haven't done that in a very long time."

"You spend your mornings with Danny Tanner these days instead?" Raquel smiled at him.

"I suppose I may have gotten a little complacent." Adam's eyes darted over to her, and he smiled back the smallest bit.

Raquel shrugged. "It's easy to do. I saw it in the hospital all the time. It's easy to see in others, but harder to recognize when it's happening to you."

As she said the words, something flashed in the back of Raquel's brain. Maybe her experience with complacency was feeling a little more familiar lately. She knew what it was like to feel helpless and trapped, and so she also knew just how vital it was to figure a way out of the maze.

"I miss the horses," Adam went on. "I rode a lot back in the day, even when my leg was at its worst. Just kind of gritted my teeth through any pain or discomfort and it was worth the effort. It wasn't until the clotting problems that I started to lay off. I'm not sure..."

His voice halted over the words. Raquel looked up at him.

"I'm not sure how to get back to it," he continued. His shoulders were shrugged down. His neck stooped.

Raquel stopped in her walking and turned to him. "That's what you hired me for," she reminded him. "Let's take back the life that you want. The independence, the horses, all of it. I'm not a great maid, but I am a halfway-decent nurse. I can help you with that."

Adam smiled. "Sounds like a tall order for such a short girl."

"I've faced worse." She shrugged and smiled back at him.

They continued in their walking, beginning to circle back to the little house. The sun was fully up now, and the air was getting hotter. The sweat at the back of Raquel's neck was picking up. She was glad for the sports bra now. She thought to herself that it might even be nice to run into town to pick up a few more. Was there a Target in Goldfinch?

Adam started fanning himself. He pulled back the collar of the robe, waving it back and forth to air out. "We're still pretty far from the house," he mused. "Would it bother you if I took off my robe? The only problem is that I'm not wearing any boxers underneath..."

Raquel stopped walking and crossed her arms to smirk back at him. "Adam Gardner, how many times am I going to tell you that no new tactic of yours will scare me off? Nudity included."

Adam put up his hands and laughed. "It was worth one more shot."

"You are incorrigible," she informed him as they picked back up the pace.

"So, I've been told," he grinned. "Alright, Florence, if I have to be awake this early, we might as well talk. Tell me about your life back in Vegas. Do you highfalutin city folk have talking robots and flying cars yet?"

Raquel snorted. "We're really not *that* different from Goldfinch," she said. "Oh! But there is this new attraction out on the Strip where you can see all this new tech that's supposed to come out next year. Apparently, there's this phone that's like an iPod with touch controls..."

They walked and talked, circling the land around the little house until the morning dew had all dried up and the animals had hidden in their cool burrows once more. Raquel was surprised by how easy it was to talk to Adam once he got away from his self-pity and snark. He was charming, funny, smart, even. She was ashamed to admit that she hadn't expected those qualities judging by the isolated, podunk nature of his hometown.

She couldn't remember the last time she'd walked and talked like this, forgetting all sense of time and place and getting lost in the conversation. Raquel was comfortable with Adam.

Maybe *too* comfortable, she thought to herself as she eyeballed him still waving around the collar of his heavy robe in his attempt to air out. She didn't want Adam to strip down fully as he'd threatened to earlier, but she had to admit that she'd been half-hoping the collar would slip down around his shoulders.

Perhaps she should limit these personal conversations with her patient. Reestablish the professional lines between them.

The rooster crowed again, jerking her back to reality.

"Does that thing *ever* shut up?" She asked. Adam burst out laughing.

EIGHT

TWELVE DAYS LATER

"TABLE FOR ONE?"

Raquel shook off the self-consciousness that crept in and shook her head yes.

"Table for one," she confirmed.

She still hated saying that. But she wasn't going to get in her own head today. Not now, not this time.

She was two weeks into her time caring for Adam Gardner, and it was going...well? He was still a grump. Like, Archie Bunker meets Mr. Heckles, only better-looking.

But he was calling her Florence, not Ratched. He was letting her give him the herbal remedies they'd spoken about back on the porch. Raquel was becoming a more permanent fixture in his home, someone with a routine and her own space, even if she still hadn't gotten around to unpacking her duffel bags yet. Two whole weeks felt like quite the accomplishment.

It was looking very possible that her new post might just work out.

Raquel slid into the same booth she'd found on her first day in town. Ida's little restaurant smelled even better than it had the first time she'd visited. What were they cooking back there? Crack?

Raquel opened up her bag. It was stuffed with mail she needed to go through, bills she needed to pay for Adam. But first, she produced a notepad and fountain pen, ready to organize her thoughts on her first week with her new patient.

She needed to come up with a better medication plan than giving him herbal remedies every now and then, and she wanted to finally get to work on making his home more accessible for someone with the walking struggles that he had. Raquel had scheduled a guy from Flagstaff to come install grab bars in the hallway later that week, and she was hoping to talk Adam into putting up some cash to convert his tub/shower combo into a step-in before the end of the month. She chewed the end of the pen, all thoughts of "Table for one" banishing themselves to that dark spot of her brain where such nasty things went.

She looked up at the sound of a plate being slid across her booth.

"Cinnamon roll, fresh fruit, and...is that a veggie juice blend?" She smiled up at Ida.

The restaurateur had one hand tucked into her apron pocket as she cocked her head in Raquel's direction. "You look like you've had a long week and need a healthy pick-me-up," Ida mused, slipping into the seat across from Raquel. "The cinnamon roll is just a given, love."

"Your chef superpower is making it really easy to want to stay here," Raquel commented as she forked up a bite of cinnamon roll.

"You have good timing," Ida mused, untying her apron to settle in. "Your grandfather just called this morning to check in on you. He's a cute feller with that accent of his. We musta talked ten minutes because I couldn't stop listening to those sexy rolled r's." She giggled.

In any other setting, Raquel might have felt odd having a virtual stranger join her for an unexpected breakfast. But there was something about Ida that provided instant comfort, like chicken soup in human form. Raquel found herself feeling compelled to talk.

"I hope he's doing okay," Raquel fretted. "With my mama being the only one around, he might have a harder time getting to all of his outings and appointments."

"He seemed fine," Ida noted. "He mostly just wanted to know how you were doing." Ida folded her short fingers into a tight ball on the table in front of her and peered over to Raquel with a wide-eyed innocent look. "And what should I have told him to that end, love?"

"You can tell him it's still my first month, you old gossip." Raquel grinned and took a bite of her cinnamon. She thought between careful bites, reflecting on the ups and downs of her first days at Gardner Ranch. There really had been quite a bit going on lately. "And you can tell him that I miss him. It's hard to be away from family, especially when life here gets... chaotic."

"I may have heard about the scene at Dr. Weller's office the other day." Ida picked up her own fork and scooped off a bite of frosting. "I figure it's my civic duty to convince you to stick around and give Adam a chance after one of his public spectacles."

"It wasn't much of a spectacle," she assured Ida between more bites of cinnamon roll. "I don't know what you heard, but Adam just needed a little space from his mother and sisters. It was—"

"A lot?" Ida provided, one gray eyebrow sliding up into a

perfect half-circle. "With so many children in that family, there's bound to be one or two Oscar-worthy moments."

Raquel nodded. "He's far from my worst patient," she said. "He's rough around the edges, and he definitely has a mouth on him. But I get the feeling he's more bark than bite."

"I'm familiar with Adam Gardner's bite," Ida said. "He can dish it no problem. But it's far easier to tolerate such sharp words when they're coming out of such a pretty mouth, ain't it?"

Raquel blushed. Ida had slipped her intertwined fists under her chin, and her raised eyebrow had somehow drifted even farther up her forehead.

"I didn't—" Raquel fumbled. "That's not—"

Ida put up her hands. "All I'm saying, love, is if he had been a young man in Goldfinch thirty years ago, he would have been a nice buffer between my Husbands Two and Three."

"Ida, please." Raquel laughed. Her cheeks burned.

"He was skinny as a toothpick right after his kidney surgery, but now he's always out working some part of his parents' ranch," Ida went on. "The boys in town say he's tryin' to compensate for his weak leg by pushing himself, but I say that his motivations don't matter long as he's doing all that farm work with no shirt and a famer's tan. Ooh-wee. No one would blame you if you were being a little more *patient with your patient*, if you know what I mean—"

"Ida!" Raquel snorted in dismay.

Her laugh was a little too loud, her response to Ida a little too animated. The heat was making its way up her neck once more.

"Believe me, that is a bad idea," Raquel emphasized. "I'm not crossing that line. Ever."

"I saw the ad his sisters put out." Ida leaned back and crossed her arms. "It was a matchmaker's post if I ever saw one. You really didn't come here looking to hook up with the hunky rancher?"

"Definitely not," Raquel assured her. "I have my own problems with men. I don't need to add to that."

She cleared her throat and recommitted herself to what she'd been reiterating in the back of her brain for a week now. "Besides," she started. "I am his nurse. There are ethical lines that I will not cross. If I'm going to help Adam Gardner, then I need to maintain a sense of professionalism."

Ida cocked her head, eyes shining. "There's more than one way to help someone heal."

"Well, I've already stooped to trying essential oils and herbal remedies, so trust me when I say I've got the alternative medicine options covered."

"Not exactly what I meant..." Ida trailed off.

Raquel opened up her bag again, hoping that if she looked busy with some of the work she brought, Ida might take the hint and drop this line of questioning. She pulled out the stack of mail, sorting past advertisements and promotional materials.

"Adam is a great patient," Raquel went on. "But I'm really not looking for anything more. I had something more once, and it ended poorly. I can't repeat that. I'd have to be cra—"

She stopped short, holding out a thick piece of burgundy cardstock.

She traced trembling fingertips over the two familiar faces grinning up at her. There was a time when she would have given anything to see Jude and Abby so happy.

There was a staple at the top of the invitation, and

Raquel flipped the paper over to find a handwritten note on the back. *Please*, scrawled Abby's curly handwriting. *I miss you*. It physically pained Raquel to read each word.

They had set a date. This was real. There would be no going back, no great epiphany that sent Jude back into Raquel's arms and Abby apologizing for all her wrongdoings.

Sweat. Numbness. Nausea. It was all coming back.

The restaurant around Raquel went dark and fuzzy as she fumbled to put the card back on her stack of mail. She wanted to get up and leave. She wanted to lay down. She wanted to do a million different things to get away from this stupid invitation, and her body wasn't cooperating at all.

"Is that a wedding announcement, love? Will you be traveling home so soon?"

"A wedding announcement..." Raquel repeated with a weak voice. Her throat felt dry and scratchy. Like it didn't want her to speak. "No. I mean, it's a wedding announcement, yeah." She cleared her throat. She hated hearing those words out loud. "But there's no way I'll be going. It's for... It's for my ex-boyfriend and my former best friend."

Headache. Fingers tingling. Heart pounding. Raquel tugged at her collar. It felt like it was strangling her.

Ida winced. "I'll learn to shut up one of these days. Didn't mean to bring up a cheater."

Raquel shook her head again. "Jude wasn't a cheater," she said. Her voice was still thin and weak. "They never went behind my back."

She could still picture them sitting across from her on the little leather sofas in her old living room, the matching pained looks in their eyes. She didn't want to think about that. Bury the memory, repeat all of her mantras. Stop, stop, *stop*.

But *engagements end all the time* didn't really apply anymore, did it?

They had been so respectful when they told her. They weren't even touching each other, though their knees were turned in the other's direction and their fingers were just a breath apart. It was like not hurting her was the most torturous and most important thing they'd ever experienced. They'd told Raquel about their feelings and then had the *audacity* to ask her if it was okay if they got together. Like they somehow needed her permission to explode her whole world.

Raquel could still remember the exact words that had gone through her head when they told her about their emotional affair. *Did Jude and I ever love each other this way?*

The ticking clock that was always pulsing in the back of her mind was working its way ever closer to that impending wedding. This invitation only further reminded Raquel that she was two weeks more along, and still only the tiniest inch closer toward feeling more confident, more self-assured, more *human* again.

Sure, Adam Gardner brought out her old sassiness and all the quick, witty banter she could want, but that wasn't going to push her over the edge into fully happy and healthy territory. Entertaining any feelings for him was just a distraction, just another roadblock to her own recovery. It wasn't enough to heal her, just enough to numb some of the symptoms.

Raquel felt the familiar panic rising in her throat as she thought about all the work she needed to put in to control these new fears and worries. She was running out of time to get herself under control.

"No hunky rancher for me," Raquel repeated. She needed to sound more confident. More convinced. "If there's one thing I'm positive of, it's that putting my heart on the line is a surefire way to get hurt again. I thought I had something good with Jude, when really there was something even better out there for him all along. I'll stick to being a nurse for now, thank you."

"No hunky rancher for me," Raquel repeated. She needed to sound more confident. More convinced. But her tongue felt thick and heavy, like if she tried for too many words she might throw up.

"If there's one thing I'm positive of, it's that putting my heart on the line is a surefire way to get hurt again. I thought I had something good with Jude..." She trailed off. Sweat, numbness, nausea. *Stop it!* She gulped. "But really there was something even better out there for him all along. I'll stick to being a nurse for now, thank you."

Ida uncrossed her arms and placed her palms on the table, studying the backs of her hands. For a long moment, she didn't speak. Finally, she stood up.

"You won't get any more pitch from me," she promised. "I just like the Gardner boy is all. I've been partial to him ever since he was the only customer with the guts to tell me that my new tomato Florentine quiche was terrible." She smiled, exposing a gummy, sentimental smile. "All I'd suggest is that you don't be so quick to cut yourself off from taking chances. Never say never, because trust me: eating crow is a lot less delicious than eating one of my cinnamon rolls."

Raquel studied the table. The sweat was subsiding. Her fingers had feeling again. But her heartbeat still sounded in her ears, heavy and foreboding. "I'll do my best."

Ida nodded and headed off for a table where an elderly couple was parked behind their menus. "Let me guess," her voice was confident. "Two eggs over easy, plus pancakes to split?"

Raquel packed up her things, hoping to make a swift exit while the restauranteur was busy.

Maybe Ida was right. Maybe she needed to learn how to take a chance or two again. Raquel's mother certainly seemed to agree with that sentiment. But taking a chance required feeling sure of one's decisions. Being sure of the path one wants to take.

And Raquel wasn't sure she'd ever feel that way again. She remembered the frozen foods aisle at Vons. Even the panic she'd felt when Mary Gardner had confessed that Adam didn't want a nurse. The ground was always shifting beneath Raquel's feet. How was anyone supposed to be sure of anything, ever?

NINE

RAQUEL HAD GROWN up hearing the phrase "fish out of water" just like everyone else. But having spent her childhood on the fringes of the eclectic and wild Vegas strip, it seemed to her that no one could ever feel like much of a stranger for long. In her town, it was someone's personal brand of crazy that helped them to fit in with all the other drunken weirdos.

On the Gardner Ranch, though, she was beginning to understand the idiom.

Adam had left her a note on the kitchen counter that he was off to the corral. Raquel had found it on her way in from Ida's, and she headed out straight away, worrying that he might overexert himself. She'd never considered changing out of her standard early-morning yoga pants and brightly colored sports bra. It was clear to her within moments of heading out to find the corral that she would have to go buy some new clothes in the near future.

The ranch hands may as well have been from another world. They were mostly gnarled old men and women, plus the occasional muscular cowboy type. They all wore a variation on the same outfit: dusty, patched jeans, plaid button-downs, weathered wide-brimmed hats, and heavy boots. They watched Raquel pick her way through the long, unruly grasses like she was an actual alien. She focused on scanning the horizon line for signs of the corral, cursing under her breath as she hurried along.

After what felt like an eternity, she spotted Adam attempting to mount a huge brown horse just beyond the gates. It was clear even from Raquel's distant spot that he was struggling. His bad leg swung awkward and stiff as he worked to sit properly. His teeth were gritted, his jawline set into a hard, determined angle.

Adam had just gotten onto the saddle when his leg gave a quick, violent spasm. He went sliding off the side of the beast, cursing with words Raquel usually heard reserved for drunken Friday nights on the Strip back home.

She scrambled through the tall grasses, waving her arms to get his attention. "Hey!" She yelled. "Stop it! Dang brambles… don't you move an inch!"

Raquel finally got to the corral's gate. She struggled with the latch, yanking the metal back and forth until she at last settled for jumping the fence. She fell onto her hands and knees and clambered to get back up and rush over to her patient.

He waved her off before she could help him up. He hobbled up to his feet, favoring the tender bad leg.

"Where's your cane?" She scolded.

"I'm fine," Adam insisted. "The cane is an aid, not an absolute necessity. Although I'm darn near sure the whole ranch thinks I've had a heart attack given the way you ran over to save me."

"If you break that leg under my care, you may very well wish you'd had a heart attack." Raquel huffed. She furrowed her brow as she circled Adam, brushing off stray grasses and hay that clung to the back of his shirt. "You got lucky. What were you doing up there anyway? Are you insane?"

Adam waved her off. He walked back over to the horse and ran a hand along its side, stroking the coarse, dark hair with a tenderness that surprised Raquel.

"I just needed a distraction," he told her. He continued to pet the animal, whose ears had flicked forward like a dog's wagging tail. Adam's mouth twitched into the barest smile. "Drinking your witch's brew helps with the pain and all, but it doesn't do much to ease the mind. After our walk the other morning when we talked about my riding, I just thought…"

He gestured to the great expanse of wild desert grasses, like the nature spoke for itself.

Raquel walked to the other side of the horse, putting her own hands on its side. Had she ever actually seen a horse in person before? She thought now that she would remember it clearly if she had. It would be impossible to forget the incredible power of this thick, rounded chest. The powerful stillness of the animal's curved muscles. The immense heat of its huffing breath on her arm.

"Best medicine there is, huh?" Adam asked her.

Her eyes flicked over the horse to him. Her face flushed as she realized that he'd been watching her take in the horse's majesty.

"No horses in Vegas?" he asked.

"There might be a show on the Strip. But I haven't seen it." Raquel shrugged as she continued to pet the horse.

The horse gave a light snort then, making Raquel jump and pull her hand back. Adam laughed and walked around to her. He produced a thick, bristled brush from his pocket and put it into her hand.

"Fancy likes you," he explained. "That's a happy sound. You should give her a brush. She'll love you forever."

Raquel stared at the brush in her open palm. After a moment's consideration, she settled for standing on her tiptoes to run it over the top of Fancy's head. Adam laughed again and stepped closer to her.

"Jeez, Florence, you're even more city than I thought."

He reached around and took her hand, guiding the brush across the horse's side using fast, wide strokes. Raquel braced herself on Fancy's side by using her other hand. She could feel the horse taking deep, steady breaths. Her stomach did a little flip as she realized that her own breathing was starting to match Fancy's. She stepped back, gesturing the brush back to Adam. Their fingers just grazed as she passed it over.

"Lord, I hate that I can't ride." Adam stepped forward, running the brush through Fancy's hair himself.

He looked the same as he had that dark night they'd shared on the porch. Raquel could see that now-familiar pain behind his eyes. That downturn of his lips.

"I'm losing my way back," Adam said, his voice small. He continued to brush, watching Fancy rather than looking over to Raquel. "It's getting harder and harder to keep going this way. I thought that maybe if I could ride, things would be..."

His voice drifted off.

Before she knew what she was doing, Raquel's hand had shot out to stop his. Her fingers lingered on his as he stopped the brush. Adam looked over to her, his eyes even sadder than she had anticipated.

"Teach me," Raquel suggested.

What are you doing?

She couldn't help it. Raquel was plugged into Adam's

dark, tragic gaze. She wanted to help him, more than just by being his nurse. She wanted to make him smile. She wanted—

"I'm sure that you've realized by now that I wouldn't be the most patient teacher," Adam said with a wry chuckle. "Didn't you see how I lost my cool with my sisters the other day? And they're my best friends."

"It's okay if you get frustrated with me," Raquel insisted. "You said you needed the distraction, right? I can provide that. I've never had a lesson, and I've got a lot to learn."

Adam cocked his head at her, taking her in. She crossed her arms and shrugged.

"I'm your nurse," she reminded him. "This is my prescription." Choosing to phrase her command this way reminded Raquel of the line she'd promised herself never to cross.

...which was certainly getting harder to remember the more that she encountered Adam Gardner in his handsome Stetson, trim dark jeans, and button-down that gaped open at the very top.

"Alright, alright," Adam threw up his arms. "As you wish, m'lady." He extended a hand to help her up into the stirrups.

Raquel put her fingers in his. His hands were rough and calloused from a lifetime of hard work, but his touch was tender and considerate. At the contact, Raquel's mind whirled back to the little burgundy wedding invitation she'd opened up over breakfast just an hour earlier. She could still see Abby's smiling face.

And Jude's.

His hands had made her feel this way once, too. Raquel swallowed hard. *Adam is your patient. He's the one paying your bills.* How many times could she repeat the mantra to herself? She should know that just because she wanted someone with every electrified cell in her body, it didn't mean that they wanted to her back. Keeping her distance was safe. Reminding herself that she had a job to do was a way to exercise caution.

As Raquel struggled to find her footing, Adam settled for slipping his hands around her waist and heaving her up onto the horse's wide back. She shook her head, trying to scrap her way back to reality.

"Alright, sit up straight. Don't forget to use your stirrups. Hold the reins low. I'll be right here if you need anything."

Adam's hand lingered on her thigh. It was placed low, close to her knee. Respectful, but still intimate. Raquel fought back a shiver.

And she knew she had to finally admit it then, even though it made her chest ache to confess it even to herself: she wanted Adam Gardner, and wished that she wasn't just his caregiver. She hadn't thought that she could feel this spark with another man since Jude, and certainly not so soon after their breakup.

Adam had his issues, and she had hers. Raquel was just as sure now that wanting him was as bad of an idea as it had been the first million times she had assured herself of that. And yet, she had to admit her feelings at last. There was something about this wounded cowboy, something that she wanted to heal and nurture and make her own. This was well beyond her simple nursing job description.

Her feelings struggled against her long-ingrained need to maintain distance and decorum. She knew what was right, and she knew what she wanted. But that didn't make things any easier. Raquel's stomach dipped and twisted as she fought between conflicting desires to take in all of Adam —his earthy, comforting scent, his dreamy eyes, his ranch-hardened arms—and to run back to his little house, lock herself in his bathroom, and throw herself into completing the step-in shower project until her fingers were battered and bruised.

Fancy's pace picked up a little, throwing off Raquel's balance. She felt Adam's hand grip her leg tighter.

"Woah, steady there," he said with a little laugh. "If Fancy bucks you off on your first try, there's a chance I'll have to be the one nursing you."

Raquel smiled down at him, wishing with every bit of energy that she had that the color of her cheeks wouldn't give her away her inner turmoil. She gripped the reins tighter, training her eyes straight ahead. Fancy's pace increased, and soon Raquel could feel a light breeze whipping her hair up around her face, cooling the hot skin of her neck.

"Adam!" She yelled, thrilled. "I'm doing it! I'm riding!"

"Yeah, you are!" Adam grinned.

He helped to slow the horse back to a walk, and finally to a full stop. Adam ran his hand along Fancy's hind quarters with admiration and gratitude. "So, what did you think of your first time riding a horse?"

"Definitely a worthy distraction," Raquel admitted. "I just wish I wasn't wearing yoga pants and a sports bra while I did it. I'm pretty sure that all your ranch hands are already making fun of me."

Adam helped her to hop down off the horse. Raquel stumbled a bit at the landing, and he gripped her hands tight to help her find her footing. She looked up at him, just as his face cracked into a soft smile.

Perhaps even more than her own feelings of attraction to Adam, this openness and kindness he was showing Raquel took her off guard. There wasn't a hint of snark to his smile.

Nothing close to resentment hiding in the corners of his eyes.

Was it possible that their little riding lesson had been a breakthrough? Had Raquel—despite Adam's great insistence that he didn't need a nurse—actually accomplished some healing? She couldn't be more surprised.

TEN

THE PAIR WALKED BACK to their home together with at least a foot of space between them. Raquel crossed her arms, hoping that they might act as some kind of magical barrier.

"You ought to give lessons," she told him. "You know, for money. If you can't be the one in the saddle, you might as well make a buck off of helping others."

Adam shrugged. "I've never actually considered that before."

"Come on," she insisted. "Those who can't do, teach. Right?"

"Ouch!" He turned to her smiling, feigning wound from the perceived insult. Adam slipped his hands into his pockets as he walked. He kicked at loose rocks in the dirt on their path. "It *would* be nice to be around Fancy more. My little sisters have been spoiling her with treats in my absence lately. She's starting to look more cow than horse."

Raquel laughed. "You should consider it."

"That would require money," Adam reminded her. "Which, as Goldfinch's resident invalid, I do not have an abundance of.

There's a reason I live at my parents' place. Sorry to break the illusion that you've been employed by Daddy Warbucks."

"What about the money Mary mentioned from training those fillies?" she asked.

"Hire a Nurse Money isn't quite the same as Buy a Corral Money." Adam smiled.

"Maybe a training school doesn't have to be that big?" Raquel mused. "Admittedly, I don't know much about the cost, but I do know that it could be really good for you."

They reached the steps up to the little house and paused, neither seeming to know which one of them should head up first. Finally, Adam gestured, a little awkward, for Raquel to walk ahead.

"Helping someone else has its own merits as a form of therapy," she mused, stopping just in front of the door. "Take it from someone with personal experience."

"It's getting harder for me to believe that anyone would break your heart, Florence," Adam said, taking the last step up to meet her. "You cook, clean, nurse, *and* you come up with small business ideas? I'm starting to think that you made up this ex-boyfriend character as a way to add some humility to your supergirl persona."

The unexpected compliment made Raquel's heart race. She glanced up at him, her eyes darting back to the ground as fast as they could meet his face.

His smile was the slightest bit crooked. Raquel could really see it then, with Adam only a breath away. He had dark purple rings under his eyes, evidence of dozens of months spent sleepless and anxious, but they gave his blue eyes a brooding quality. And he smelled like the fresh hay from back near the corral and old leather...

Raquel's breathing was quickening again. "Um, trust me,

there's no need to tack on any extra humility," she assured him. Her voice came out stammering and unsure, as it always used to. "I'm no supergirl."

Adam opened the door for her and gestured inside. "After you."

She should wave goodbye for the afternoon and head back to her room. This was more than enough familiarity with her employer for one day. Raquel should—

"Got any thrilling afternoon plans?" She asked him. Her stomach clenched on instinct. Stupid, stupid, stupid.

"Jeez, where do I begin?" Adam walked over to the kitchen and opened up the fridge. He pulled out a cold bottle of water and held it to his forehead. "If my mother doesn't come by to check on me in person, I'm sure she'll call. Can't miss that. I've got a 5:30 appointment to lay on my bed and stare up at my ceiling. If there's time after, I'll twiddle my thumbs. Maybe play a round of Solitaire."

"Nope," Raquel shook her head. "Not Solitaire. As someone who hails from the card capitol of the world, I've got to veto such a lonely game. Come on, we'll play black-jack together instead. Maybe even poker later if you're up for it."

Adam's eyes widened. "Alright, nurse. You're in charge."

She followed him over to his kitchen. "Cards?"

"Drawer by the sink."

Raquel found them and they sat down across from one another at the tiny dining room table. "What are we betting?"

"Articles of clothing?" Adam snorted at his own joke.

Raquel cleared her throat. "Very funny. You didn't scare me off my first day here, you're not going to scare me off with a little salaciousness."

"Who said I'm still trying to scare you off?" Adam protested.

Raquel shifted in her seat and had to clear her throat. He was doing it again. Was that just Adam being Adam, the same brash, loudmouth that Ida had loved so much? Or was he—no. He couldn't really be flirting with her.

"It's like a million degrees here in Goldfinch," Raquel said. "Wouldn't it be more of a punishment to put clothes on than take them off?"

"Alright, Florence. You're on." Adam agreed. "I've got a coat closet by the door filled with all my siblings' unused winter clothes. You've got a game."

"I'll deal. We'll take turns." She smiled.

This would just be a friendly little game. Quick, easy. Like she had told Adam, there were more ways to heal than just medicine, and maybe this is just what he needed to relax a little and get out of his negative headspace.

Or at least, that was the story she was telling herself. Raquel couldn't allow herself to think that this game was anything more. Besides, she had only been in Goldfinch for two weeks. She had been with Jude for years: she knew well that relationships were supposed to take time to form, time to stabilize. Two weeks was simply too fast to form a real connection. Right?

Raquel had placed her purse on the kitchen counter before grabbing the cards. She spied it now, the tip of that burgundy invitation just peeking out. Nope. Adam couldn't be flirting with her. They had only known each other for two weeks. This was all in her head. Refocus. Recommit.

Raquel dealt out the first hand, keeping the cards in neat order for Adam to play. He made a big show of checking under the table to make sure she wasn't hiding any cards.

"I'm not a cheater," she assured him with a laugh.

"I can't trust you," He narrowed his eyes, faking suspicion. "You're practically a stranger."

Raquel handed him his next card, which he pulled back and hid to himself.

"You don't have to keep it from me," she laughed, reaching for him to put his cards back on the table. "That's not how this game works—"

Adam smiled, a quick, fleeting expression, as he pulled the cards farther away from her. "Told ya I can't trust you."

"Wow, that was the biggest tell I've ever seen," Raquel snorted. "And I spent a summer in high school working Harris Casino, where all the drunks play. You should feel lucky we didn't start with poker." She played her own card face down. "Hit?"

"Mock me all you want, but I've spent a lot of time in a lot of hospital rooms perfecting my card skills," Adam bragged as he continued to motion for play. "You can just—"

"Yikes, that was a fast bust." Raquel smiled and waggled her eyebrows. "I believe there's a trench coat in the closet with your name on it."

Adam's eyes widened with surprise. Nevertheless, he got up from his seat and picked out a giant coat. He pulled it around his shoulders, its fur-lined hood standing up around his ears.

"New round."

"Deal." Raquel smiled. "Hope the doctor is okay with all the weight you're gonna lose in sweat, Mr. Gardner."

"Bring it on, Florence."

They dealt again, and Adam won the next round. Raquel donned a hand-knit poncho and they continued.

"Alright, hit?" She asked again.

"Hit... hit.... TWENTY-ONE!" Adam grinned as he pointed to the closet for Raquel to grab more winter clothes. "I should take up counting cards. I think I'm a natural."

"And very cocky," Raquel added. She slid on a thick pair of gloves and fumbled to deal new cards. "We'll just see how this continues. Hit?"

Adam motioned with one hand, very cool. His grin widened as he won another round. "Is it really cockiness if I have the God-given ability to back it up?" He winked.

Adam was getting competitive. He was full-on bouncing in his chair now; it was the most expressive that Raquel had seen him since she had arrived in Goldfinch. They played game after game, and he won most of the rounds. He was confident and boastful, razzing her over mistakes and shimmying with happiness in his victories.

Raquel didn't mind though. Her own smile was wearing out her cheeks, leaving her face tired and stretched. She had noticed how Adam limped less on the few occasions that he walked over to the coat closet. He sat up straighter at the table. He never commented on any pain.

"You look really hot," Adam said.

"I—what?" Raquel shook her head to clear it.

"Your cheeks are all red," he replied. Adam got up from his spot. He pulled the cards into a neat little pile and crossed over to her chair. "I think that's the end of our game."

"Oh, come on!" Raquel protested. "I think you're getting scared. You finally pulled a bad hand, and now your luck is catching up with you."

"Florence, you have on four layers of coats, my father's ski pants, and a beanie." He snorted. "Let me help you out of all that."

"Ugh," Raquel groaned. "Fine. But I expect a rematch soon."

"Deal." Adam smiled as he helped her to stand up from the table.

He worked off the arm of one of her coats, then the other. Together, they worked with care to shimmy off the layers and place them back on their hangers.

"I can take the last one off myself," she said, unzipping the polyester. She tossed the last coat to Adam and threw her arms up in the air. "Free! Man, I hadn't realized how hot I was until now."

"Consider it your official welcome to a desert summer." Adam grinned. He stepped toward her. "But, uh, you forgot the hat."

He reached forward and slipped it off her head. Raquel could feel the way her dark locks were matted to the sides of her face. Her ponytail was damp at the base from where she'd been sweating. She felt a bead drip now, working its way down between her shoulder blades and making her shiver at the tickle.

Adam was only a breath away. Raquel had to tilt her head up to look him in the eyes.

"Um, I suppose I ought to start filling out some of those forms for your upcoming appointment," she stammered. "Work calls."

"Sure," he agreed. "Good idea."

But neither of them made a move to leave.

Raquel felt paralyzed in her spot in front of him. He was so handsome it almost hurt to look at him. And so funny and clever. He seemed to enjoy her company. She wanted him.

But at the same time, she felt an all-too-familiar rush of ice in her veins. There was a terror lurking just beneath her skin, that thing that had given her panic attacks and night-mares and made her want to swear off falling for another man ever again. Putting aside the fact that the man she was currently attracted to was her patient, could Raquel ever summon the courage needed to put her heart on the line again? She had been so sure of Jude once, and he had chosen someone else. She had given everything she had to another person and been let down. Could a human being survive something like that twice?

And yet, Raquel couldn't help but wonder if maybe—just maybe—she had a shot with him. Maybe she could want him and he could want her back. Maybe she could allow herself to feel happy again, to heal her patient and herself and to take full advantage of this fresh start in Goldfinch.

Certainly, there would be some time in the future where she was no longer Adam's nurse and he was no longer her patient. She'd heard of coworkers back at the hospital dating their patients, usually at least a year after their last appointments. Christa Long had even married a guy she met in the E.R. It was possible. There were ways that Raquel could make this work ethically and emotionally, if she decided that she wanted to put herself out there again and take these last few vital steps toward healing.

Sure, Abby and Jude's wedding was coming, but maybe Raquel could have made some serious progress by then after all. Maybe she could finally feel sure that she was worthy of someone else's love and affection, and, further-more, that she was a whole and complete person on her own.

Her heart was racing. She felt her feet move just an iota closer to Adam. She could smell that grassy scent again, the deep-aged leather...

They jumped apart as the phone went off on Adam's kitchen counter. Adam winced.

"And, that would be that daily call from my mother," he said. "I wish I had been kidding about that."

"I'll be in my room," Raquel told him. She retrained her eyes on the floor, hoping that he wouldn't notice how red her cheeks had surely gotten.

She headed off down the dark hallway. Raquel knew that she would probably waste a fair bit of time before she started in on the paperwork she had mentioned. She would roll around on her bed, stare out the window, think once more about the hurt she had experienced.

But deep down, she already knew that she'd made a decision. If she was going to preach healing and persistence to Adam Gardner, then she ought to take her own advice. Raquel still needed to be cautious with him. He was her employer, he had a past with drug abuse, and most importantly, he was still her patient, at least for the foreseeable. But maybe she'd been wrong.

Was there any shot that she could love and be loved in return?

ELEVEN

"OKAY." Mary Gardner rolled up her shirt sleeves as she assessed the mess of boxes and packing peanuts floating around her childhood bedroom. She bit her lip as she decided what she wanted to do next.

"Claudia, you can help me sort through my stuff," she continued. "Raquel, Adam: you're both on box packing duty in the hallway. Please try not to use up a whole roll of packing tape like you did last move, *Adam*. And Grace and Sarah, do you two mind doing the heavy lifting to take my things out to Claudia's car? Don't want to reinjure our resident invalid here and get stuck paying for his medical bills in addition to my new rent."

She stuck her tongue out at Adam. "So considerate of you, sister," he teased.

"My pleasure," Mary grinned back.

"Better get on it," Mary's friend Claudia mused. "Matt's coming to move in here in the morning, right?"

"Let us not speak of that tragedy," Mary said with a dramatic hand to her heart. "It's hard for me to imagine my older brother sleeping under my Edward Cullen *Twilight* poster. This used to be a safe space."

"Hold it together, woman!" Grace laughed as she and Sarah picked up the only two fully packed bags and started out toward Claudia's truck. "You're the one who went out and got her own apartment; the room was his to take!"

"Whose side are you on?" Mary mumbled. She walked into her old bedroom and returned with a haphazard armful of scarves and hats. "You two can start in on these," she told Raquel and Adam. "Claudia, let's turn on some music and get started."

The girls disappeared into the bedroom, leaving Raquel and her patient alone in the hallway. The loud beat to a No Doubt jam started to play through the door.

Raquel couldn't help it—as tall, dark-haired, and gorgeous Claudia left to help Mary pack, she felt a small breath of relief. Had she been… insecure about another woman? Jealous, even?

"Tape or box duty?" Adam asked her, interrupting Raquel's taboo thoughts with a gesture of clear packing tape and a mound of folded cardboard.

She placed her hands on her hips, pretending to take the decision very seriously. "What a thinker," she said. "Gimme the box. I hate struggling with that sticky packing tape."

"Wise decision," Adam said with a smile.

"So," Raquel started as they found their positions around the mound of Mary's accessories. "Come here often?"

Adam laughed out loud. Raquel smiled; she liked the easy way it sounded. "Matter of fact, I do," he laughed again. "This is our second family move this year. Matthew's move-in tomorrow will make it three."

"Who moved last?" She asked.

"Me," Adam said. Raquel felt her eyes widen as he looked up at her. He smiled, looking a little sheepish. "I know, I know. My place is so messy and ill-kept that you probably thought I'd been living there for years."

"Definitely not," Raquel assured him seriously. "Doesn't everyone move into a new house and immediately start collecting old Pepsi cans and Wal-Mart bags?"

"You got me there." Adam laughed again as she sealed up their first box and he placed a line of tape over the opening.

"Why did you move out anyway?" Raquel couldn't help but ask the question. "If you were living here with your parents before, wouldn't it have been easier and cheaper to just have them check in on your health stuff? I'm sure the house could be made a little more accessible. It would have been a breeze."

"Ah, yes, and I'm sure that being the almost thirty-year-old cripple living with his mommy and daddy would have brought in all the beautiful nurses without any help-wanted ad required." He smiled.

Raquel's response was split in too many directions at Adam's joke. There it was again, the armor of snark and self-deprecation that Adam had clearly used to get by for years, and buried in there was a compliment to her. Maybe even a —*don't think it don't think it don't think it*—flirtation? Raquel cleared her throat and tried to ignore the way the tips of her ears were burning.

"What was your turning point?" She asked him.

"I don't know that there was any *one* turning point," Adam replied. His eyes were losing focus as he ran tape over the same line he had before. He was faraway, thinking back to somewhere else. "It was a series of sunrises, each more beautiful than the last. Maybe I wasn't as hopeless then.

Maybe I just didn't watch as many *Full House* reruns because my younger siblings hogged the TV. But back then, I was watching those sunrises every morning, and all I could think about was how much I wanted some part of that frontier to be all my own. I wanted my own corner of land, my own horses, my own dirt and weeds and trees."

Adam's eyes flicked up to Raquel's and her breath caught in her throat.

"... My own family." He looked down, busying himself with the box folds. "I can't have all that if I'm stuck here forever. I needed to move forward. Stop treading water. Moving out was a necessity."

Raquel picked up their finished box and moved it down the hallway for Grace and the other Gardner sister, Sarah, to come retrieve. She brushed her hands off on her yoga pants as she returned to Adam's side.

Mary burst through her bedroom door with several drawer's worth of folded clothes. She set the garments on the floor in front of them and gestured wildly. "I can't give any of 'em up!" She announced. "Claudia tried to talk me into a Goodwill run, but I cannot be persuaded. Sorry in advance."

She disappeared back into her bedroom. Adam and Raquel both shot each other a *look*, chuckling together over Mary's dramatics. They picked up a new box and tape and started in on loading it up.

"You know, I can relate to you," Raquel offered as they pressed shirts into the bottom of the box. "I had pretty similar motivations in moving out here to work for you."

Adam raised an eyebrow. "More boyfriend stuff?"

"More boyfriend stuff," Raquel confirmed with a sigh. "I had to get away and start over. I needed some place that was all my own."

"It's terrifying, isn't it?" Adam asked her. He had set down the box and looked at her with open, curious eyes. "No one tells you that adulthood is full of so much risk and self-doubt."

"...I cried in church the Sunday before I took the bus to Goldfinch," Raquel admitted with a small laugh. "I was a big baby."

"Please, I dialed a phone sex hotline on my first night alone in the new place just to have someone to talk to that wasn't my parents." Adam grinned. "Always remember: my life is sadder than yours, Florence."

"I had a panic attack in the grocery store, like, a month ago," Raquel told him, planting one hand on her hip and smiling cockily. "Ice cream exploded everywhere. Clean up on Aisle Party-of-One."

"Woman, my ma ushered the Seventh Day Adventists to my front door in an attempt to get me to finally see some other human beings."

They both laughed.

"So if Mary slept here, where was your old room?" Raquel asked, peering down the hallway.

"Upstairs," Adam explained. "But don't get excited for me to give you the tour. My parents wasted no time turning it into my nephew's new playroom. They had moved in a massive stuffed Barney before I had even packed my first box."

"Now, see, if you had taken someone like me home from a date and I had seen that massive Barney in your room, I would have been totally enamored." Raquel grinned.

Adam's face shifted, crinkling into a coy smirk. "If I had taken someone like *you* home from a date?" He repeated.

Raquel immediately felt a wave of light-headedness as she realized her poor choice of words. She stammered, fidgeting with an unyielding cardboard box as she tried to figure out what to say next. "I, um..."

"I mean, I would have thought for sure that a date like you would have preferred my menagerie of hamsters," Adam supplied for her, grinning. "Or perhaps my extensive collection of Agent Scully posters from *The X-Files*? I mean, between that and my sexy limp, I was like catnip for cute girls growing up."

"Shut up!" Raquel looked up, smiling back. "I had two different posters of Mulder on my walls growing up. *The X-Files* was basically my introduction to absurd science fiction. I couldn't get enough of the monsters, so I turned to the hard stuff from *Mystery Science Theater*."

"Ha!" Adam laughed out loud and put a hand on his hip. He cocked his head, the crooked little smile widening as he sized her up. "You catch *Starship Troopers* a few years ago?"

"In theaters. I saw that *Logan's Run* is playing in the drive-in out at the edge of town—"

"Saw it twice before you got here." Adam grinned again. "I'm glad we're learning these things about each other now, Florence. I think I'm more comfortable with a nurse as weird as I am."

"You bet," Raquel smiled at him. "Now 'the truth is out there.'"

In another part of the house, a landline went off. Neither Raquel nor Adam made any motion to go answer it. Raquel felt frozen in place, smiling up at Adam like it was the easiest thing she'd ever done. There it was again—that now-familiar feeling that if she only just reached out a little bit, she might touch him. She might... kiss him.

The phone started up blaring again.

"Is anyone going to answer that?" Mary came out of her

room huffing. "I've been waiting on a call from my new landlord."

She jogged around the corner and disappeared.

"Maybe it's not the worst thing that you're working here, Florence," Adam told Raquel, still staring down at her with the crooked little smile. He was hardly a breath away.

"We can certainly commiserate with one another," Raquel agreed.

"I've been looking for someone to watch all those terrible sci-fi movies with," he said, the smile getting bigger. More mischievous. "It's not as fun to do the commentary alone."

"I can do that," she breathed.

"And it's nice to have a ranch newbie. Someone who can be my horse-riding test subject."

"I can do that, too."

Adam stepped closer. Their chests were practically touching. Raquel held her breath.

"And maybe, if you're real nice, I can show you—"

"Raquel, it's for you!" Mary rounded the corner, her arms crossed and face sour as she gestured a phone with a long curly cord.

"For me?" Raquel turned to her, puzzled, feeling a little off-kilter.

"Some chick named Abby," Mary shrugged and offered up the phone again. "Says she got this number from someone in Vegas?"

The heat flamed over Raquel's cheeks. She took a step back, as though the cord from the phone might jump off of the wall and strangle her if she got too close.

"I don't want to talk to her," she said, shaking her head. "Just hang up."

"It's Abby?" Adam asked. "As in—"

"Yeah," Raquel confirmed, her voice weak. "As in *that* Abby."

Adam walked over to his sister, took the phone, and placed it to his ear. "Try again later," he said, before jogging around the corner and slapping the phone back on its cradle.

He returned to the girls, sliding an arm around Raquel's shoulders. She was surprised to realize that she was shaking —more than the rumors around Vegas, more than the wedding invitation with the hand-scrawled note, *this* felt too close. Too personal.

What was perhaps even worse was how much she wanted to go back to that phone and call Abby back. She wanted to reconcile with her friend, to hear Abby's chipper, high-pitched voice giggling as they laughed about how silly all of this had been. Raquel wanted normalcy back. She wanted it more than anything.

Adam pulled her around into an unexpected hug and she buried her face into his shoulder. He felt so strong. So safe.

Okay, Raquel admitted to herself. Maybe everything new wasn't all bad.

TWELVE

"I'M TWENTY-SEVEN," Adam reminded Raquel as they walked over to his parents' ranch house. It was a week after Mary had moved out, and Matt was now moving in. "I live alone. I have even had a dog all by myself once. I'm a grown man."

"Correction, you live with a nurse now," Raquel smiled over at him and picked up the pace. "Because you are a kidney transplant patient with recurring health problems and a limp."

They reached the sliding glass doors to the Gardners' living room, and Raquel stopped. She put her hands on her hips and cocked her head at him.

"I also have it on very good authority from your sister that Bingo ran away when he was under your care," she said. "So this grown man will accept his nurse's help in moving his little brother so that he doesn't end up living in a hospital instead."

"Has anyone ever told you that you're bossy?" Adam groused as he pulled back the door.

"No," Raquel remarked with a laugh. "At least, no one has told me that in a very long time."

It was true—he brought it out in her. This sassy, funny side of Raquel that made her feel confident and charming. It was a feeling that she had been leaning into for days now, ever since that moment at the blackjack game, when she had realized how much she wanted Adam. She wasn't going to live in fear again. Running away from risk was no way to spend a life.

"I promise, I'd be fine without you," Adam assured her. "Transplant patient, limp, runaway dog, *whatever*, I know my limits."

"I'm not so convinced yet," Raquel smirked. "I saw how you hopped up on Fancy earlier this week with no regard for your healing." She cleared her throat. "Which reminds me, I've got some stretches we'll start doing tonight. See if we can get that leg to stop swelling so much. Maybe we can set aside some time after I give you your injections and pills?"

Adam rolled his eyes. "See, you had me interested when you mentioned a pretty girl stretching my leg, but you lost me at 'injections and pills.'"

A low rumble crackled in the distance. They both turned in the doorway. Adam examined the horizon as he leaned on the cane he'd taken with him. The sky was choked with dust, but the air was dry and pressing.

"Hope that was just thunder and lightning from the heat," he muttered, a concerned crease forming between his eyebrows. "Otherwise, it's a bad time to be unloading a U-Haul."

They slipped inside.

"Hey, you made it over!" A tall, lanky young man with hair as blonde as Adam's called over to them from the other side of the room. He set down a large cardboard box he was carrying and jogged over.

"This is my brother, Matthew," Adam explained. "Matty, this is—"

"Raquel," Matthew supplied. He rolled the R in her name and winked. "Good night, nurse! Adam is lucky to have you."

Adam rolled his eyes but laughed. "Alright, just point us to which room they have you in—"

"Don't let the fact that I'm moving back into my parents' house fool you," Matthew jumped in, sliding his arm around Raquel's shoulders. Adam crossed his arms as he watched, head cocked and eyebrow raised. "It's only because I broke up with my beautiful, supermodel ex-girlfriend, and I figured they needed a little companionship. Speaking of which, do *you* need a little companionship, Raquel? I'm sure it's hard living under the same roof as the lesser Gardner brother. Do you have to change adult diapers for him? Hide his pills in peanut butter?"

"Alright, that's enough." Adam pulled his brother over and put him in a headlock. Matthew grinned and took it, pretending to put up a struggle.

"Don't you scare off Florence," Adam lectured Matthew. "She's a good egg."

Matthew laughed and went jogging off to collect the box he'd left on the floor. Raquel felt her stomach tighten and release as the exchange ended. *She's a good egg.* She liked to hear Adam say that.

"Truck should be parked around front," Adam told her. He gestured for her to follow him down a hallway. "You sure you're up for this?"

"Bring it on," she grinned.

They started to leave the room, but they were stopped by a teenage boy with the signature Gardner blonde hair.

"What the heck, Adam, you brought a *girl*? I'm totally going to shame Ruth about not coming to help Matty move. She said it was a 'boy's only day.'"

"I swear, she said she'd give me the wrong meds if I didn't let her help." Adam threw up his hands as they passed. He turned back and gestured to Raquel as the boy rounded the corner into the living room. "Jacob, this is Raquel!"

Jacob waved to her with one hand as he disappeared into the next room. Raquel waved back, feeling a little overwhelmed by all the greetings. Adam mostly kept to his secluded corner of the property; even after a few weeks of caring for him, she hadn't met anyone more than Grace, Mary, and Esther.

They reached the front door, and Adam opened it for her. Raquel turned up to look at him, eyes wide. "I think you Gardners have enough blondes to populate Sweden."

"You have no idea."

The sky had darkened further in the brief moment they had spent indoors. Adam hobbled over to the U-Haul, his limp pronounced as he moved to meet an older man heaving a tower of balanced boxes down a ramp.

The wind picked up, whipping locks of hair loose from Raquel's ponytail. She pulled her cardigan tighter around her shoulders and squinted her eyes in a desperate attempt to keep dust out. The trees lining the front drive were alive with the gale, their thin leaves quivering. They made a noise as they shook, like tiny wings flapping.

"Think it'll rain, Pa?" Adam called over to the man at the U-Haul.

"Lord, I hope not." The Gardner patriarch glanced up at

the threatening sky, his face screwed up with worry. "I told Matty we needed to get this done earlier. I'm hoping it's just a haboob."

"We'll just have to work fast, I guess." Adam waved to Raquel and she jogged over. The wind was picking up even more as they stood there, and she had to shield her eyes as she waved up at Adam's father.

"I'm Raq—"

"I know who you are." He smiled. "Sam Gardner. I'd shake your hand, but I think we're running on precious seconds here."

"Where did y'all put the dolley?" Adam asked Sam. He was near-yelling over the bluster.

"Mary's old room," Sam answered. "But I'm not sure there's a spare minute to roll it over. We're running out of—"

As he spoke, a streak of blue-white lightning ripped through the sky. It was followed by a spattering of fat, heavy drops, which escalated in a blink into a full-on torrent. Sam covered his head with a slab of cardboard. His white work shirt was already soaked through. He gestured like a madman toward the fields behind them.

"Adam, the horses!"

Raquel turned, her hair whipping and sticking to her lips and cheeks. She could hear the horses now. Their whinnies were a loud cacophony of complaint over the low, rumbling thunder. Adam pushed past her, staggering along with a hurried gait, his shirt collar pulled up over his ears.

"Hey!" She called out, scrambling to run after him. "Wait for me!"

She tailed him over to the horses. He turned back to her with the briefest glance as he let himself into the corral. "They're not scared," he assured her. "Just looking for shelter."

"The horses weren't the ones I was worried about," she hollered over the rain.

Raquel wasn't sure he heard her though. Adam was moving at a breakneck pace, his limp pronounced but seemingly ignored by him. She stood back, trying to herd the animals out of the barn with him, but feeling useless.

She wasn't sure she'd be much help anyway—not with the way that he looked now. Raquel could hardly see Adam through the rain, but what she did see made her stop in place. His blonde hair had been smoothed down like a sheet against his skin, hugging jutting cheekbones and sharp jawline. His shirt, too, clung to his body, making him appear slick and lithe. In the downpour, Adam almost appeared as one of the horses he was corralling: something primal and brute.

Terrifying to behold. Impossible to ignore.

Raquel followed him to the safety of the barn. The horses scattered from the tight circle they had formed outside, meandering away to the comforts of their individual stalls. Adam was dripping, shaking his head out like a dog as she approached.

She pushed him in the chest. Maybe it was the storm, maybe it was the desire that she hadn't felt in so long... she couldn't say for sure. But she felt a surge of emotion. Something powerful, stirring.

Her fingertips were tingling. Neck sweating. Heart pounding.

"You could have been hurt out there!" She scolded him. "I'm here to help you! Let me do that!"

"I'm fine, Florence," he assured her. He smiled at her. The crooked angle to his cherry lips only incensed her further.

"Don't ignore me!" She insisted. "I'm not going to let you

get hurt."

Raquel went to push him again, but Adam caught her wrist in the air and pulled her toward him. "I could tell you the same thing."

The dizziness was back in one overwhelming rush. The sense of panic.

Raquel hesitated, sensing the connection that was coming before it could happen. For a moment, she was completely paralyzed, frozen between all that she had fought to protect and all that could still yet be.

But then, in a rush, she felt desire propelling her forward. Sweat, heartbeat, tingles. Headache, chills, dizziness. Sweat, heartbeat, tingles, headache, chills, dizziness. Sweat, heartbeat, heartbeat, heartbeat heartbeatheartbeat- heartbearthearbeat—

She surrendered to the feeling and Adam pulled her close, tipping her chin up to his as he kissed her deeply. She clutched at his wet shirt like it was a lifeline. Tiny drops wrung out into the hay from the pressure of her fingertips.

When it was over, he kissed her forehead and rested his chin on top of her wet hair. Raquel could hardly breathe. She was lost in the smell of him. Her body was buzzing with sensation.

Instinct told her to take a step back. To walk away. But she squeezed her eyes shut. Everything was different now: there was no going back. All that worry about ethics. Guarding her heart. Playing it safe. It had all been thrown out the window with one impulsive kiss. Raquel couldn't get back that safe little shell she'd carved out for herself, at least not the same way as it once was. She was changed. Irrevocably. It was earth-shattering. Terrifying.

Exhilarating.

"I don't know how to do this," she whispered.

Her voice was almost inaudible over the din of the storm. And yet, it was clear he understood. Adam nodded and pulled her closer against him.

"Neither do I," he whispered back. "But I'm willing to take a gamble if you are."

THIRTEEN

THE NEXT MORNING, Raquel beat Ida to the restaurant. It was still dark outside when she got there; she'd slipped away after Adam had left to help Matthew finish setting up his bedroom.

Ida had stopped short in the parking lot, a coffee and set of keys balanced in one hand and a binder overflowing with bills in the other. Her eyes had gone wide when she took in Raquel's tight, excited smile and her bouncing from the ball of one foot to the other.

"Ay, love," Ida clucked to herself as she stepped by Raquel and inserted a key to open up the place. "It's a Bloody Mary morning I see."

"I'm sorry to get here so early," Raquel stammered, following her inside. "I wasn't sure where else to go. Something happened last night. In fact, I feel silly and embarrassed to admit—"

Ida slid behind her counter, opened up a cabinet under the register, and whipped a bottle of vodka onto the counter.

Raquel balked. "Ida, I know people say 'It's five o'clock somewhere,' but 4 a.m.? Really?"

Ida put one hand on her hip and sassed her customer with a very matter-of-fact glance. "So does Adam Gardner taste like chewing tobacco, love? That's always been my one complaint about kissing these farmer boys."

Raquel's jaw dropped open and Ida grinned. "But if I'm off base, I'm happy to keep the Bloody Mary mix in the pantry."

Raquel laughed out loud. A hand flew to her forehead in amazement. "... More like sweet bubblegum actually." She grinned.

Ida howled with laughter as she opened the bottle and pulled out two glasses from the same cabinet.

"Honestly, how did you know that I kissed Adam?" Raquel didn't wait for the Bloody Mary mix to come out. She knocked back a shot as soon as Ida poured it, her head still whirling from the madness that was the night before.

Ida shrugged and smiled. "It didn't take a lot of luck to guess that the slap-happy grinning girl on my restaurant porch at 4 a.m. had man-related news. Now if you don't start telling me all the details, I'm afraid I'll have to cut you off. This is the expensive stuff you're drinking."

Raquel slid onto a stool across from the register and groaned. She rested her face on her open palms, letting her hair fall forward like a curtain between them. "We kissed once in the storm—"

"Mmm," Ida purred. "That was a good one last night."

"...And then a bunch of times after that when we got back home."

"Ha!" Ida trilled. "Don't worry, I'll hold back those saucy details when Diego calls about you this morning. He's been asking to hear about my home improvement plans anyway."

"Abuelo called again?" Raquel asked, surprised.

"Darn near every morning." Ida's cheeks flushed pale

pink. It was the first time since Raquel had met her that she looked anywhere close to bashful. "But tell me more about Adam! You can't distract me when there's good gossip afoot."

Raquel felt her own cheeks burning. "He's wonderful, Ida. I feel like I'm in a dream. I went from sad and despondent to the stuff of romance-movies almost overnight."

"Eek!" Ida squealed and danced back and forth on the balls of her feet.

"It's not smooth sailing yet," Raquel told her. "We had to have a talk about our professional relationship and that still leaves me feeling a little icky. I made him agree to stop paying me if we're going to be more than friends. Free rent, free utilities, free food at the ranch... I'd say that's still a fair deal that won't make me feel like some kind of call girl."

"Mmm, details, details... It would seem that the Gardner sisters' ad for a nurse was really for a mail-order bride after all." Ida laughed to herself as she refilled the vodka. "Well, you better have a darn good reason for being here with me pre-sunrise and not back at home cuddling the sexy rancher."

"Ugh, I'm still not sure how to go about that," Raquel explained. "Even after kissing on the couch for a while, I made it clear that I was heading to my room and he was going to his. When he popped by before sunrise to tell me that he couldn't sleep and he was going to go unload more boxes for his brother, I had to pretend like I was totally fine before sneaking over here and unburdening my soul."

"Why would you have to pretend that?"

"Ida," Raquel put both hands on the counter. She steadied her breathing and thought back to the words she'd been rehearsing to herself all night in the dark as she stared up at her ceiling. "I'm his nurse. Technically, he's my boss. Logically, I know that getting involved is a terrible idea... even if I've been trying to logic this away all night long."

"Don't tell that to my line cook, Angelo," Ida winked. "I've finally got him right where I want him."

"Ida, I'm serious!"

"So am I!" The restaurateur insisted, shrugging. "You've already kissed. You know he cares for you and you care for him. What is there to lose in going after what you want, love?"

Raquel's stomach clenched. There was a lot to lose in going after what she wanted.

She paused for a moment, working to slow her breathing. To somehow will the sweat that had pooled on the back of her neck into submission. She took another sip of the vodka before looking up at Ida again.

"You know, if your superpower is guessing your customers' orders, mine would be remembering them," Raquel shared, biting her lip. "I've got an incredible sensory memory. It served me well back in school. I was always at the top of my nursing class when it came to practical skills."

Raquel took another sip. Her fingers were shaking, triggering a flash of the frozen foods aisle at Vons Grocery Store. She steadied the glass with her other hand, cupping it between her fingers.

"So even though I started dating my ex, Jude, almost four years ago, I can still remember exactly what it felt like in the beginning," she continued quietly. "How good it felt to kiss him. How much I wanted him. How much I *thought* he wanted me."

She cleared her throat. Ida extended a hand as if on instinct. She took Raquel's palm in her own and squeezed, infusing her with the last ounce of courage she needed to continue to unload.

"So that's how I know what there is to lose in going after what I want," Raquel explained. "Because the last time I really went all in for something, it ended with the guy leaving me for my best friend. My whole world exploded around me because I'd been too blind to see that things weren't perfect to begin with. And, this time, with Adam—" Raquel sighed, thinking back to that late night conversation they'd shared together out on the porch on the second night she'd been in Goldfinch—"he comes with baggage of which I'm already well aware. To add our complicated employment relationship on top of that is just asking for trouble."

Ida stayed silent, her brow furrowed as she watched Raquel.

"Right?" Raquel pushed, waving her hands in the air. "I mean, *shouldn't* I be hesitant?"

Finally, Ida put one hand on her hip as she pushed aside the glasses and vodka bottle with the other. "That's it; I'm cutting you off this morning."

Raquel groaned and ran her hands through her hair. The gesture did nothing to clear her racing mind.

"Come on," Raquel started. "You've been so quick with the advice before. Can't I get anything from you this morning?"

Ida reached across the counter and took both of Raquel's hands in her own. Her round cheeks grew rosy as she fiercely locked eyes with the young nurse. "You like Adam Gardner?" She asked her.

"Yes," Raquel admitted.

"More than just finding him attractive, right?" Ida pressed. "I mean, I'm sure that *helps*—"

"Yes, *yes*," Raquel quickly cut her off with a laugh. "But it definitely helps."

She could see Adam helping her to ride Fancy for the

first time. Playing blackjack with her. Laughing over the weird herbal remedies she had him try. There was more there than the wet t-shirt or the tanned skin. A lot more.

"Then, by calling upon my special chef's superpower to always know what the customer needs, my recommendation is that you kiss that boy again," Ida pronounced, pulling her hands back to cross her arms with pride. Raquel started to jump in with protests, but Ida cut her off with a finger. "Adam Gardner is not your ex-boyfriend Jude. And you won't know if he'll break your heart unless you give him a chance to do so."

Raquel's eyes fell to the countertop again. Her heart was beating so loud it was hard to hear herself think. She shouldn't have had that vodka.

"Ida, I don't know if I can survive that again."

"It's hard, love." Ida crossed around the counter and slid a meaty arm around Raquel's shoulders. She pulled her close. Raquel breathed in deep the scents of bacon grease and brown sugar that seemed to have seeped into her clothing. Ida wasn't her mother. Her restaurant wasn't Raquel's home back in Vegas. But it felt darn close.

"Try again, and maybe this time, things will be different," Ida told her. "Take a risk. Go for what you want. And if Adam Gardner dares to break your heart, then you'll know which Goldfinch restaurant owner has the ability to poison his breakfast."

Raquel smiled at that one.

"And until then, be sure to kiss him as much as possible," Ida added. "I wouldn't be opposed to hearing about a little necking and petting, too."

Raquel laughed and elbowed Ida in faux-horror. Ida ambled back around to the other side of the counter, pulling out a box of silverware to start setting up for the morning.

Meanwhile, Raquel continued to sip at the remnants of her vodka as she sat and thought. She couldn't help it: she wanted to believe what Ida said. She wanted to keep on kissing Adam and falling for him and seeing where this exciting new road in Goldfinch led her. It was terrifying, sure, but she knew that a part of her ached to see what this life had to offer.

Ida was right. Adam wasn't Jude. Maybe this time could be different. Maybe this time could be better. Raquel polished off the vodka and slid the glass back across the counter. *Take a risk,* Ida's voice repeated in her mind. *Go for what you want.*

FOURTEEN

THREE DAYS LATER

THE CELL PHONE had been ringing for days.

It wasn't Miriam calling Raquel. And Diego was too busy calling Ida to call another number. Raquel knew who was calling before she ever had to even look at the number.

ABBY.

This morning, she'd stuck it under her pillowcase to drown out the annoying vibration. When that didn't work, she'd brought it over to one of her still-packed suitcases and ditched it in a front pocket. The buzz still haunted Raquel, though, like the beating of a darn tell-tale heart. She sat at the edge of her bed, every muscle tense as she wondered what Abby had called to say. Raquel still had the wedding invitation stashed at the bottom of her purse. Maybe she needed to hide that thing better, too.

Why did she have to be former best friends with someone so insistent and stubborn? She was starting to hear her phone ringing even in her dreams...

A knock sounded at the door and Raquel jumped. She got up to open it and found Adam standing in the hallway. He held his cowboy hat to his chest and looked up at her with those signature impassioned blue eyes. Raquel felt her breath catch in her throat; the invitation and the cell phone were all but forgotten.

"Do you have a second?" He asked. Despite all the kissing they'd done a few nights prior, he still hung back from the door frame. With his hat held like that and his innocuous, hopeful expression, Adam looked like a gentleman, a sharp contrast from his usual sassy punk persona. "There's something I'd like to show you."

"Definitely," Raquel nodded. She grabbed a baseball cap from her nightstand and tugged it on. "Let's get out of here."

She followed Adam out of the house. The day was bright and hot, all evidence of the recent thunderstorm completely eradicated from nature's memory. Raquel had to shield her eyes as they picked though long grasses and headed over to the corral.

Fancy was tied up to a post and waiting. She gave an excited whinny as Adam waved in her direction.

"Okay, so I've got all your equipment set out here. You can borrow Grace's riding helmet and breeches. I went out and bought a nice new bridle and saddle for Fancy this morning. A saddle pad, too. I signed up for an open clinic, and as of one hour ago, I've applied for my 7-day certification course. We're all ready for trial lesson number one."

Adam looked back over to Raquel, the pride on his face evident. He was rocking on the heels of his boots, unable to contain his enthusiasm.

"Trial lesson number one?" Raquel repeated.

"I know, it's not my own corral," Adam shook his head and took a few steps away, new frustration settling in. "I can't afford that yet. But I figure I can train folks here on the weekends and get a legitimate business going, right? I know it's not impressive. I know it's not even that professional yet, but—"

"Adam," Raquel cut him off. She smiled over at him. "I love it."

His face split into a grin. He took a hesitant step in her direction, sliding one hand around the small of her back as he pulled her close to kiss her gently. There was a caution to his touch, unmissable. It only endeared him to Raquel further; she could relate more than he knew. She was reminded of just how nervous Adam was to go after what he wanted, too. How many risks stood between him and a return to the life he wanted more than anything. Raquel let her hand work its way up the back of his neck and into his hair. She wanted this kiss to go on forever.

At last, she pulled away, smiling. "I can't believe you pulled all this off. Watch out, Goldfinch, there's a new small business owner in town to take all your money."

"Ugh," Adam rolled his eyes and elbowed her playfully. "Don't get all sappy me on me now, Florence, or I'll ask one of my siblings to be my first trial lesson instead."

She laughed and rolled her eyes back. Adam took her hand and guided her toward Fancy. "Okay," he started as he helped her to suit up. "I know you only rode for the first time the other day, so I figured that this time we could launch into something that requires a little more skill."

He helped Raquel to get back up on the horse as she had the first day. Just as she had felt that first ride, she noticed the soft touch of his hand on her leg. The gentle, patient way that Adam helped her to find her balance. He really would be a good teacher. It hadn't been Raquel's worst idea.

"Alright, Florence, you ready for the big leagues? We're gonna trot."

"Trot? Was that not what we were doing before?" Raquel clutched the reins a little bit tighter.

Adam laughed. "You were barely walking!" He told her. "Maybe it was just getting lost in my irresistible smile that made you *feel* like you were moving faster than you were."

"Oh, please." Raquel stuck her tongue out.

"Okay," Adam focused up and ran his hands over her riding boots. "You're going to start out walking, then close your calves in at the same time. Hang on tight, and I'll show you how to properly dismount when you're done. Think you can manage?"

"On it." Raquel nodded. They set off around the corral and her fingers clutched tighter to the reins on instinct. It was so high up on Fancy's back. She felt an unexpected sense of awe that Adam had been able to ride the way that he had been several days ago with his bad leg.

"You're doing great," Adam smiled. "I'd say this was a win. Ready to try the dismount?"

"Sure thing, partner," she said.

Adam groaned and laughed. "You are so city it hurts."

"Be nice to me, or I'm never giving your horse back," Raquel teased. "You taught me how to ride her, so I'll drive her all the way back to Vegas and you'll never see either of us again."

"I'm glad to see that your teacher has instilled so much confidence in you," he replied with a smile. "Alright, put one hand at the neck and one hand at the saddle, please. You're going to lean forward now, and kick your leg back and over. Then, you can jump down and—"

Adam winced as Raquel slid down the saddle, her clothes catching and causing her to stumble back and fall to the ground.

"You okay?" He pulled her up and brushed off her jeans.

Raquel nodded. "Guess that's the reason for a doing a trial lesson?"

"Yep," Adam agreed. "Here, I can just show you the right way myself."

Raquel marveled at the way he pulled up onto Fancy with ease. There was something so natural about his movements, so intuitive.

Adam set off with confidence. He pulled his calves in tight just as he'd told Raquel to do, and Fancy set off into a beautiful trot. Raquel clapped her hands and cheered.

"Yeah, yeah," Adam brushed her off, but smiled, too. It was clear that he felt good up there. She hoped he was getting some small taste of the life he missed so much.

Adam guided Fancy back over to Raquel, slowing the horse to a full stop.

"Alright," he said. "Now watch me dismount. Pay careful attention to the way that I jump down and away from the horse. I don't slide down. That's a recipe for bruised ribs."

Adam kicked his feet from the stirrups. His body pushed up and he started to swing his right leg around.

"Argh!" Adam's voice came out choked and pained as his leg caught at the last second, ripping away from his body at an odd angle. He slid down the rest of the way, just as he'd told Raquel not to do. He collapsed into a heap on the ground, his teeth gritted and eyes squeezed tight as he babied his bad leg.

"Adam!" Raquel rushed over to him.

He put an arm up to stop her. "I'm fine," he promised, beginning to push himself up from the ground. "Really, I'm —" But he was cut off by a fresh wave of pain.

"Let me help you," she instructed him. Raquel got down in the dirt next to him, examining his leg for new injury. "It's swelling up a bit, but I think it was just the weird angle that's giving you pain. You're going to want to lay off for the rest of the day. I can walk you back to the house."

Adam nodded. "Sounds like a plan," he agreed through tight lips.

Raquel wrapped an arm around him and helped him to push up off the ground. He was heavy and broad, and she had to grit her own teeth to muster up the strength to help him. Together, they worked their way out of the corral, shutting the gate behind them before heading off toward Adam's house.

They walked in silence. Adam was quiet as he tried to stomach the pain of hobbling back to his home, but for Raquel, it was different. Her mind was racing and her stomach churning.

It was her fault that he had been up on that horse. It was her fault that he'd gotten hurt.

Raquel had been so stupid. She'd gotten sidetracked, lost in those baby blue eyes and the sweet rancher's drawl. She'd pushed Adam too far too fast. He should never have been out riding Fancy; if Raquel had been a smart, attentive nurse she would have insisted that Adam stay home and get some bedrest. A little case of the *Full House* blues wasn't the worst thing in the world if it meant that he didn't risk further injury.

She glanced over at Adam as she helped him tackle the stairs back up to the front door. His jaw was a hard-set line, the sweat on his brow was picking up in a heavy sheen. Lord, he was handsome. She felt silly checking him out like this. And he was funny and hard-working, too? *Come on.*

Raquel needed to step it up and do her job as his nurse better. That was priority one. But she couldn't allow herself to take too much of a step back from Adam quite yet. She wanted him too badly. She was in too deep.

Maybe this time she really could have everything she wanted. Maybe she could learn to strike a better balance between practicality and the dizzying effects of her new emotions.

Maybe.

FIFTEEN

"I THOUGHT Christians weren't big on drinking alcohol?" Raquel smirked as she propped up Adam against her side and led him into their house. She was getting used to serving as his human cane.

Adam barked with laughter, his eyes big and shiny, his smile sloppy. "I thought *you* weren't big on drinking alcohol."

"Ooh, good comeback." Raquel teased.

It had been a true accident. The day after Adam took Raquel for a practice lesson was family Bunco night. They'd made mocktails, with some of the older sisters and Esther sipping on real appletinis and cosmos. Adam had been off alcohol for years, as it was too much of a trigger. But when he'd picked up the wrong drink and shotgunned it to take his nightly maintenance meds, he'd set himself up for a doozy of a recovery evening. His coordination and speech were the first victims of the accidental combination.

"Seriously," Raquel asked. "How did you not taste so much tequila?"

"I was distracted by a pretty girl sitting next to me,"

Adam explained, his face somber and serious. "A pretty girl who was cleaning out my pockets of every last penny…"

"Hey, you knew I was a Vegas girl when you hired me! Gambling is in my blood." She grinned as they took the steps up to the house.

"Where was this girl when we played blackjack the other day? Were you hustling me, Villa… Valley…Voyo…" He slurred over the words, like his lips wouldn't obey his brain. "Dang it, why does your last name have so many syll'bles in it?"

Raquel laughed. "You're cute." She stood on her tiptoes and kissed him on the nose.

Adam grinned. "Mmm, that's the stuff."

"Alright, Barney Gumble, let's get you in bed."

Raquel opened the door and they stumbled through. To her surprise, the living room light was on. She blinked into the yellow haze, wishing she hadn't had her own glass of wine back at the game night.

"Hey."

Raquel jumped at the sound of the familiar voice and stepped on Adam's boots as she backed away.

"Ouch! Dang, Florence, I'm drugged, not dead!" Adam joked.

But she didn't really hear him. She was too focused on the unexpected visitor who was standing up from Adam's living room couch.

"What are you doing here, Abby?"

Raquel's ex-best friend trained her eyes on the floor and dug the toe of her Converse into the patterned area rug.

Beside Raquel, Adam stiffened up like Abby's presence had suddenly sobered him up. He turned to Raquel, putting a gentle hand to her elbow. His eyes widened: *you gonna be okay*? She nodded in his direction and motioned for him to leave them alone. Adam stumbled a bit down the hallway, feeling his way in the dark and casting worried glances back at his nurse and her late-night visitor.

"I'm sorry," Abby started. She sucked on her bottom lip as she tried to think of what might be best to say next. "I tried calling you, but you weren't picking up. I got this address from your abuelo, and when the door was unlocked and no one was home, I took a chance—"

She took a hesitant step in Raquel's direction, but Raquel held up a hand to make her stop. "Stop," she instructed. "Don't come any closer. I can't do this right now." Her tone was a lot more timid than confident, but Raquel did her best not to let her face betray her fears.

Abby hung her head and rubbed the back of her neck. Her expression looked so pained, her dark brown eyes so full of feeling, it almost hurt Raquel to look at her. She forced herself to look away from Abby, to remind herself of the friend who had betrayed her rather than the sad, pleading woman who had come all the way out to Goldfinch to talk with her.

"I have no right to be here," Abby said, her voice hardly a whisper. "I know that. I'm not stupid: I know that even though Jude never cheated, I still did something very wrong with him. I broke something sacred between you and me. That can't just be fixed with one visit to Arizona."

"You're right," Raquel agreed curtly. "It can't."

"You asked me what I'm doing here," Abby started, her voice halting and cautious. "The truth is I'm not sure. I'm not sure of anything without you. I hate this, and I hate myself. I know now that if it comes down to it, I would choose you again every time. Jude might be my boyfriend... but you're my soulmate."

Raquel wanted to be mean. She wanted to cut Abby with

her words, to make her feel as empty and lost and tortured as she had felt for the past several months.

But it was difficult. Abby had always been the confident friend, the one who knew how to take what she wanted and had the courage to actually do so. Now, though, Abby's whole body was hunched over with nerves and sadness. Raquel could see that her nailbeds had been picked raw from the habitual chewing she resorted to on the rare occasions she got nervous. She stood pigeon-toed and awkward; her whole being screaming discomfort and uncertainty.

Raquel wanted to stop her from feeling this way. She wanted to erase the pain that had lain dormant between them, pretend like the past several months had never happened. For the first time maybe ever, Raquel was beginning to understand how it must have felt for her best friend and her boyfriend to have to sit her down and tell her the worst news of her life. It was waking torture.

It must have taken real commitment. A real sense of assuredness about their feelings for one another.

"I put more work into my relationship with Jude than I have into anything my whole life." Raquel struggled to get the confession out, to give voice to what had tortured her for so long. She could feel her own neck hunching as she revealed this deep, intimate part of herself. The words that she had never had a chance to speak aloud to her best friend before. "I made changes to who I was. I modified myself, worked to make myself the very best I could be for him. And it wasn't enough."

Abby bit her bottom lip harder and nodded. "You were incredible," she said. "Jude still speaks so highly of you. He misses you. We both do—"

Raquel put up one hand to stop Abby. She squeezed her eyes shut; she didn't want to hear about how highly Jude might speak of her. She didn't want to know how much he missed her.

"You know, when you two sat me down and told me about your feelings for one another, the betrayal hurt. But that wasn't the worst part." Raquel cleared her throat, working up the nerve to give voice to the scariest thing she had been carrying with her. "The worst part was how happy you looked. You were still Abby, he was still Jude, and neither one of you had to make a single change to who you were to be the best for each other. All that work I did to better myself, all the late-night conversations and reading relationship books from the library... it was all pointless. I was never going to be right for him, and I felt like an absolute idiot for having ever deluded myself into believing that I could be. The embarrassment was worse than the betrayal by far."

The dark irises of Abby's eyes shone bright with glistening tears. She nodded, her hands fidgeting against her abdomen. "I was wrong to come and try to mend things," she admitted. "But I'm planning this wedding and—it's not that I expected you to be in it, I'm not insane—I just missed you. I hate that it was Jude I fell in love with. I hate that the price of my love story was losing my best friend." Abby gathered her purse from the living room coffee table. "I'm so sorry, Raquel," she said again. "Thank you for letting me say my peace."

She started toward the door, but Raquel reached out a hand to stop her. Her fingers still clutching the light fabric of Abby's sweater, Raquel looked her old friend dead in the eye.

"The embarrassment was bad," she started, her voice small and cautious. "But even worse has been losing my best friend, too."

Before she could fully comprehend what she was doing, Raquel was pulling Abby into a stiff, mechanical hug. It wasn't the soft, open gesture they'd practiced a million times before in their friendship. It was rusty, robotic from dormancy. And yet, it dissolved into something more real and intimate with each passing moment, and soon, Raquel found herself holding the back of her friend's dark head as Abby sobbed into her shoulder, her hands clinging to her jacket. Abby smelled like their Vegas home: vaguely smoky and cocktail sweet. Familiar. Raquel breathed it in as she pulled back, resting her forehead to her friend's.

"Lord, this is so awkward," Raquel breathed. Out of long-engrained habit, she shut her eyes as if that might shield her from the discomfort.

"...It is," Abby admitted wryly. "But I hope it gets better."

"Soulmates," Raquel agreed with Abby's sentiment from earlier. "Even when I really wish we weren't. And trust me, I've been really, *really* wishing that for the past few months."

Abby laughed at that, a half-choked sound as her newfound joy battled with her tears.

"I'm not sure how to navigate this," Raquel admitted with a small smile.

"Who cares?" Abby let out another tiny laugh. "I'm just glad we're going to try at all."

"I can't believe you came all the way out here." Raquel finally pulled back and walked over to collapse onto Adam's couch. Abby crossed over and sat opposite her. "That long bus ride was almost enough to make me second guess taking this job."

"I wouldn't know," Abby shrugged as she wiped away the last remnants of her tears. "I hitchhiked."

"You did *not*." Raquel was surprised, and yet she could easily picture Abby on the side of the road, her thumb stuck out nonchalantly as some chicken truck rolled up to offer a ride. Typical. Had it been that long of a time apart that she'd forgotten all these little intricacies that made up her best friend?

Raquel stiffened as she more fully considered Abby's hitchhiking anecdote. "What about Jude?" She asked, her voice catching over each word. "Didn't he want—"

"He told me he'd drive me out here, but I figured that was a bad idea." Abby looked down at her hands, still uncomfortable talking openly about the shared man in their lives. "You might be a quiet one, Villanueva, but I'd still rather face off with Ted Bundy than with you when you're livid."

Raquel flashed a wry smile. "I do get a little feisty when I've been wronged. Or, at least, I used to." It was nice to remember a time when she wasn't so plagued by trepidation and anxiety.

As odd as it was for her to think of Abby as she once was, it was even more odd for Raquel to consider her former self yet again. With Adam, she was only just getting to that point where the panic attacks were fading behind her. For the first time in a very long time, she was beginning to feel more like she had in the past. More confident. Happier. Like that feisty Latina best friend that Abby had just referenced was still inside her, ready to emerge victorious when the moment finally came.

"Is it too early for me to make a joke about that new patient you're treating?" Abby's eyes darted down the hallway in the direction Adam had disappeared. "Maybe you had an easier time moving on than I would have thought."

They made eye contact, and Raquel felt her face turning red. Abby's own cheeks flushed in response. "Oh jeez, I'm so sorry," Abby apologized. "I think I'm just desperate to bridge over the awkward Jude gap between us. Turns out I'm not good at it."

Raquel looked down at her folded hands and took a deep breath. Over four months of silent treatment and yet Abby had nailed down Raquel's feelings within five minutes of being together again: she really hadn't had much time to wallow over Jude when Adam was around flashing those baby blues and pulling out the rancher charm.

Still, the comment made her want to shut down. It made her want to push Abby back through the front door so that she wouldn't have to think the romance or her job or anything complicated ever again.

Raquel set her shoulders, firming up her resolve to let Abby back in. If they were going to be friends again—if that countdown calendar to Abby's wedding date was ever going to finally, *finally* disappear from Raquel's brain—then it was going to take a few awkward jokes and emotional admissions to get there.

"I may have gotten a little more with this job than I thought I would," Raquel admitted. "Adam Gardner is... well, he's really something."

Abby smiled, suppressing what Raquel figured was one of her signature happy squeals. Abby and Jude weren't off the hook yet; both girls knew that only time could repair that damage fully. But talking about a new boy, new possibilities... this could be one step closer to their old sense of normal.

"Thank God for that," Abby said, looking genuinely relieved. "I'm so happy for you. Is it moving fast? I mean, aside from the obvious: you already live together." Her wide mouth spread into a smile at her cheeky joke.

Typical Abby, ready with a one-liner even after all this

time apart. But something about the crack stirred something in Raquel.

Maybe it was just seeing Abby after all this time, maybe it was talking so much about Jude after months of careful silence. But whatever it was, a flash of memory jolted through Raquel's brain: unpacking her bags in Jude's bedroom. Picking out new furniture for their living room. Painting the walls of their apartment together.

Raquel shook her head, trying to clear it. She smiled. "It's all very PG with Adam," she informed Abby. "He's a devout Christian and a real gentleman cowboy. Or at least, a gentleman cowboy with a smart mouth."

"Well color me very impressed that you two are keeping it PG when he has a face like an Abercrombie model," Abby gushed. "Tell me he's not brainy or funny, too? That can't be legal."

"If I tell you Adam's a good conversationalist, will you come after him, too?" Raquel teased. Abby looked taken aback for all of a split second, before Raquel tossed a pillow at her face and laughed. Just a few minutes back together and they were already joking and making fun of each other. Even about the big stuff. Maybe there was hope for their friendship after all.

"But really," Raquel continued. "You should have seen us tonight at his family's game night. A guy hasn't made me laugh that hard since—"

Her voice faded off as she remembered well the last time a guy had made her laugh that hard. It was the time before, when she hadn't known about Jude and Abby. They'd gotten together in the little apartment kitchen and tried to make homemade pizza together. Jude had thrown the dough up to toss it, and it had gotten stuck on top of the refrigerator. Raquel had teased him about it all night and for the rest of the weekend. They'd laughed about it intermittently for days after.

Abby didn't seem to notice the distracted quality to Raquel's face or the way her voice had faded off. She was too distracted by how happy she felt to be with her old friend, how jazzed she was that things were finally returning to normal.

A crash sounded from down the hall. And then, Adam's warbly drunken voice, "I'm okay back here!"

Both of the girls dissolved into giggles, all memories of Jude and the apartment and Raquel's old life tabling themselves in a safe space for the time being.

"Tell me you're not staying in town," Raquel told Abby. "There's, like, one motel there, and I'm pretty sure it's haunted."

"Honestly, I didn't have a plan." Abby sheepishly tucked a rogue ringlet back behind her ear. "I was just kind of winging it and hoping for the best."

"That won't do," Raquel shook her head. She stood up and offered her hand to help Abby up. One more step: *be brave.* "You'll stay in my room. I mean, I obviously need to check with Adam first. It's his house. But I think we've got some catching up to do."

Abby took her hand, interlocking their fingers. It felt good to Raquel. It felt right.

"Okay," Abby agreed. She stood up and slid a duffel onto her shoulder. "Better to head to your room now anyway. I have a *lot* of questions about Hotty McRancher over there. You two seem perfect for each other."

"Alright, alright," Raquel appeased her with a smile. She gestured down the hallway and followed Abby down toward her room, planning to check in with Adam when he was a little more sobered up.

Again, there was something about what Abby said that stirred something up inside of Raquel. Something that left her stomach feeling sour and unsettled. It wasn't her best friend's visit that had left her in turmoil, but rather something that Abby had pointed out after their long time apart.

You two seem perfect for each other. The more she repeated the phrase in her head, the more Raquel started to add emphasis to the word "seem."

She'd been so happy with Jude. They'd taken all the right steps. They'd enjoyed one another. Said their "I love yous." Raquel had been happy. She had thought their life together was perfect. And she'd been very, very wrong.

Would the other shoe eventually drop with Adam, too? At what point did *seeming* perfect fail to translate to an actual love story?

SIXTEEN

SOMETHING WAS VERY OFF.

It wasn't rekindling her friendship with Abby; about that much, Raquel was sure. She had three days to think it over as Abby stayed at the little ranch house and tagged along for errands, doctor appointments, and everything in between. The pair had picked up like nothing had ever happened between them. After Raquel's nursing duties, they stayed up late watching bad sci-fi movies in the living room, tried to cook some of the country recipes from Adam's family cookbook, and Abby even got her very first horse riding lesson.

But her presence at Gardner Ranch struck a chord with Raquel. It was too familiar. She didn't want to be threatened by Abby spending time with Adam, but there was still a level of concern lurking in the background. It was a trigger, a trigger that was pressed every time that Adam cracked a joke that made Abby laugh, or helped Abby up to a ride or horse, or invited Abby along when he and Raquel headed into town.

Raquel tried to stay logical. She heard Abby's hushed phone calls with Jude every night from the back room. She knew that they loved each other, a reminder which was one part relief and one part pain. Furthermore, she knew that the odds of Abby swooping in on her man a second time—especially after the way they were still fighting to regain their friendship—were slim.

Raquel had gone full lizard brain, her instincts around Adam falling away from the trust they'd built and into something more primitive and suspicious. For the three days that Abby was in town, she hardly slept. Her appetite dropped off. The cold sweats returned. The numbness. The nausea.

The haunting phrase that Abby had uttered that first night kept replaying in Raquel's head: *You two seem perfect for each other.* She dissected every word of the sentence, picking it apart until the words didn't even sound like English anymore. She and Adam *seemed* perfect for each other. But were they?

Before they knew it, it was time for Abby to leave. Wedding planning called, a fact which Raquel still felt a little awkward about, but more sad now that she considered missing out on such a vital part of her best friend's life. The trio loaded Abby up into Adam's truck and they headed to the bus station. He'd insisted on paying for her ticket to ensure that she not bail on the bus station at the last second in favor of hitchhiking again.

"You're robbing me of a cultural experience," Abby said, eyes sparkling as she stepped up to the bus stop.

"Is Goldfinch not cultural enough for you, Carrie Bradshaw?" Adam smiled back and nudged her forward. His nickname for Abby had come as naturally as "Florence" had after he spent a late-night watching *Sex and the City* reruns with the girls. It made Raquel's stomach clench to hear it used.

Adam slung his arm around Raquel's shoulders as Abby stepped up onto the bus platform. She leaned into his warm body, trying to get lost in that rugged hay and leather smell she loved so much.

"Call us when you get back in town," she instructed Abby.

"I will," Abby smiled.

"And—" Raquel's voice caught just a little "—tell Jude hello. For me."

"I will." Abby nodded. Her eyes searched Raquel's with the quickest movement, as though unsure that this was reality. At last, Abby reached forward and gave Raquel's hands one final squeeze before heading up the bus steps and disappearing behind the window.

The bus doors shut. Adam and Raquel waved up where Abby had poked her head out. The vehicle groaned, its whole body creaking as it pulled away from the station. Raquel felt her breath quicken, and she waved her last goodbye as the bus rolled around the corner and carried her best friend back to Vegas.

Adam pulled Raquel around to the front of his body, holding her close. He looked down at her, the top of her forehead only just clearing his chin.

"Abby's gone," he announced. "You know what that means. I'm going to start roaming the halls nude after my showers and playing my Michael Bolton CDs on blast."

Raquel elbowed him. It brought instant relief to hear him cracking jokes meant just for her again. "I already told you, Gardner, there's nothing you can do to get rid of me now. Nudity included."

"Get rid of you?" Adam balked, eyes sparkling with mischief. "Florence, that was clearly flirting."

Raquel allowed herself a laugh as Adam led her back to

where his truck was parked in the lot. The pace of her breath hadn't come down since Abby boarded the bus and it was still quick now, leaving her feeling a little too light on her feet.

"I've got a surprise for you back home," Adam announced as they pulled out of the lot.

"Jeez, a surprise?" Raquel turned to him, eyes wide. "What is it?"

"My lips are sealed." He grinned. "You'll have to wait and see."

They took Main Street home. Raquel stared out the window as Adam chattered on, her breathing getting ever faster. Her mind flashed back to the frozen foods aisle.

There was nothing to feel anxious about. Raquel had reconciled with Abby. She had a steady job. She had an incredible man by her side, someone who had planned a surprise for her and teased her about how much he wanted her around. What *real* reason could there be for her breathing this way? Raquel sat on her hands, hoping she could stop her fingers from shaking. *Breathe.*

They pulled up to the little house. Adam got out of his side quickly and trotted around, limp almost imperceptible, to Raquel's side before she could get out. He opened the door and gestured for her to exit.

"My lady," Adam said. "After you."

Raquel walked through the dust and rocks up to the front door. She pushed it open, scanning the living room like there might be a monster waiting inside.

"Is the surprise that you cleaned up for the first time while I was gone to breakfast with Abby?" She smirked and raised an eyebrow.

"I did channel my inner Danny Tanner," Adam admitted. He grinned. "But that's not the surprise. After me."

He held out his hand for her to take.

The quick breathing returned full-force. Adam looked so open. So kind. Like the only thing he wanted in the world was to surprise Raquel and make her happy.

She felt a stab in her chest, then a razor-sharp feeling that spread through her body leaving the taste of metal in her mouth. She wanted him so badly. Too badly. Merely taking his hand now and following him to the back of the room felt dangerous. Like she was stepping too close to a fire...

Raquel took his hand anyway and followed him through the dark hallways toward her bedroom.

"I hope it's nothing too big or fancy..." Her voice was warbling.

Adam turned back to her, grinning. He rocked on the heels of his boots as they arrived just outside her closed bedroom door. "Oh, come on," he started. "You can't go saying 'nothing big or fancy' because it will set up what I did to look small-time and lame."

"Well, at least tell me that you didn't spend any money, right?" Raquel asked.

"Not a penny," Adam smiled again. He reached down and squeeze her fingers. "It's just a little something I did while you were out to brunch with Abby. I saw the way you were with her. Even after all the time apart, it's clear that she's a little piece of home. And I wanted to give you a taste of that here."

He turned the door handle and pushed it open.

Raquel stepped forward into a wonderland of glimmering lights. Adam had strung tiny, twinkling bulbs around the antique furniture and curtain rods. They beamed back at the couple like glittering fairies, illuminating the boxy room in a dreamy yellow haze.

But, even more important than the lights themselves, was what they were clearly supposed to highlight. Raquel's two duffels now sat on her bed, unzipped and splayed open, their contents removed. She turned to the nightstand: there were her glasses, her current mystery novel. On the dresser was her small collection of perfumes and makeups. In the open closet, she saw hanging her few shirts and yoga pants.

Adam pushed past her, back to the room, his face split from ear to ear with a happy grin. "Surprise," his voice was soft and breathy. He squeezed her fingers again. "Welcome home."

Sweat. Numbness. Nausea.

Old symptoms came racing back to Raquel, and she stumbled a bit, bracing herself against the door. She thought the right words to reply, but none of them were coming to her mouth. Her tongue was heavy and dry. Her throat was gummed up and cottony. She managed a small smile, but found her feet fumbling back through the doorway anyway.

Adam reached forward and pulled her close. "Is it too much?" His eyes were wide and worried. Vulnerable. "I'm so sorry. I can take it all down. The lights were in our Christmas storage. I thought they might remind you of the Vegas Strip lights is all. It would take five minutes to undo them."

Raquel shook her head, trying her best to reassure him. The haze around the twinkling lights was getting thicker now. Their contrast to the rest of the room growing starker as Raquel's world grew smaller. She was breathing fast. Too fast. A tiny sound escaped her lips, and Adam took it as affirmation.

"I know it's fast," he said. His eyes searched the ground as he looked for the right words. "I know it's scary. I mean,

I'm a transplant survivor and you're still probably the scariest thing I've ever faced. But I want this, Raquel. I want you, I want us, I want you to be a part of my life and have a real home here. I want to do it all for you. Because the truth is—"

Adam's eyes flicked up then, searching out Raquel's own. Her knees were going weak. She struggled to stay standing.

"The truth is I love you." He kissed her then, one hand slipping into the back of her hair to hold her tight.

Raquel wanted it. She leaned into the kiss like it was a lifeline, like it was the only thing that could keep her tethered to the here and now.

But the more she fought for Adam, the more Raquel felt herself slipping far back and away. Her breathing was too fast. It grew more and more shallow, worsening the more that he held her lips to his.

Headache. Fingers tingling. Heart pounding. It was all familiar. It was all too much.

And then, before Raquel knew it, the room had faded to black. The last thing she remembered was the flashing of the tiny Christmas lights strung up over her windows. As she blinked on her way down to collapse in Adam's arms, she could have sworn that she saw the lights flickering and fading, too.

SEVENTEEN

"I'M FINE, I PROMISE!" Raquel covered her eyes in embarrassment as Adam set her down on the couch. "Wouldn't my bed have been more practical anyway?"

Adam rushed over to his kitchen, pulling out a rag and running it under cool water. He was wheezing from the exertion of carrying Raquel's limp body down the hall and to the couch. She winced as she thought back to how he'd appeared as she glanced up at him, having started to come round from her fainting spell. Adam had looked so determined, so protective.

"Nurse Florence," he lectured, placing the chilled rag to her forehead. "You know very well that the kitchen is where we keep all First Aid supplies and much-needed comforts. Your own highly organized system forced my hand—I *had* to bring you to the couch if I wanted to take care of you the Raquel Villanueva way."

Adam grinned, but Raquel's stomach twisted tighter in return. She hated that she had put him in the position of needing to take care of her. She was *his* nurse, *his* caretaker. Raquel's anxieties about her budding relationship with Adam had forced her into another panic attack, thereby forcing him to pick up her slack. The incident only further reinforced what she was already beginning to suspect: just because she loved someone and wanted things to work didn't mean that their romance was written in the stars.

She'd learned that the hard way with Jude. She wasn't sure that she could learn it all over again with Adam.

Raquel's mind flashed back to one of her first breakfasts with Ida, when she'd insisted on keeping her distance from her new patient and sparing herself from any potential pain. Had she been right?

If she was being honest with herself, Raquel had to admit that she didn't want to be correct. She wanted everything to be as good with Adam as it felt. She wanted their chemistry and easy banter to translate over into a healthy, happy relationship. Something long term. Something she didn't have to worry about. But between her anxieties and his own problems... Raquel just couldn't feel as sure as she would like.

Her attentions were pulled back to the present as Adam flipped on the ceiling fan and crossed back to her. He rested the rag over Raquel's forehead in one delicate motion and then slid down to her feet to prop them up on a couch pillow.

"You passed out, Florence. You are *not* fine." Adam was scolding her. He sounded the vaguest bit angry, even. But as he got down on his knees next to Raquel's spot on the couch, she could see terror in his eyes. Primal distress.

He shook his head like he was trying to clear his face of any betraying emotion. He smiled down at her, running his fingers through her hair. "You must be throwing back that rancher food," he joked. He was out of breath and coughed a little. "Darn near killed me to carry you down that hallway to the couch."

"You shouldn't be tending to me," Raquel scolded him right back. "I had a little fainting spell. Doesn't that just make me a classic gentlelady like Scarlett O'Hara or something? You have your own meds to take and your oils to apply. I swear, I can't even remember the last time you took them. I've really been slacking. Don't let me get in the way of that."

Raquel felt a an even deeper stab of guilt in her chest as she said the words aloud. Adam *did* have his own regiment to get back to. She was his nurse, and yet, here he was, the one taking care of her. They hadn't been able to balance both, as Adam had insisted when they'd first kissed. There were lines between patient and caregiver for a reason, and Raquel had stomped all over them in her haste to be sweet with the one good looking boy who'd paid her any attention. The thought made her feel dizzy and ill all over again. She rubbed her hands over her face, trying to get a hold of herself.

Adam replaced the pillow under her feet by sitting down and propping her legs on his. "That's nonsense," he told her. He grabbed the remote from the side table and flipped on the TV. "We're just going to have to put tonight on pause and watch *Crocosauraus Rex 3* on Sy-Fy. I know the right medicine for a night like this."

He grinned over at her, a rogue lock of his white-blonde hair flipping down over one eye to make him look like an impish teen. Adam flipped over to the right channel. It was clear to Raquel that he was trying to make light of the situation, but his brow was still creased with worry.

But as much as the guilt was eating at Raquel, she still couldn't help but want to assuage Adam's fears. On instinct, she snuggled in tighter to his body. She pulled a blanket up over their legs and smiled at him.

"I really am fine," she repeated. "I promise. But cuddling you and watching a terrible sci-fi movie does sound like a good fix for the evening." Here she was, still unable to get enough of him.

"Excellent," Adam announced. He squeezed Raquel's knee, making her jump and laugh. "And if a bad movie doesn't do the trick, I hear that a little light kissing works wonders."

He gave a cough, and she wiggled away like he had the plague.

"Stay back, sicko!" She laughed. "You're terrible, Mr. Gardner." A smile had pulled onto her lips involuntarily.

"You love it, Florence." He smiled back.

Raquel sat up suddenly, a small rush of dizziness returning. "Adam…" she started, hesitant. "What have you been eating?"

He laughed. "Tell me that my diet doesn't matter in this new health routine," he groaned. "I can't give up my nightly beef jerky. I'm farm stock, after all."

Raquel reached forward with shaking hands. This time they weren't quivering from quickened breathing or a sense of unidentifiable panic. She ran her thumb over Adam's smiling bottom lip. It was blue. Undeniably blue.

"Seriously," she repeated. "You didn't steal a popsicle before you dropped off Abby with me or something?"

"Do I look five years old?" He raised an eyebrow.

Raquel shook her head, trying to clear it. "When was the last time you took your anticoagulants?" She asked.

"My blood thinner?" Adam asked, the smile fading into a look of puzzlement. His face screwed up with thought. "When did Abby come into town again?"

Raquel could feel her blood freezing in her veins. "She stayed for three days."

"Three days?" Adam repeated, frowning. "Jeez, I can't believe that. I guess I got a little distracted by everything going on. It got kind of crazy around here, didn't it?"

Even the short remark had caused his breath to quicken. Raquel could tell that Adam was starting to notice, too. He put a hand to his chest like he felt a pain there and cocked his head, going quiet. He opened his mouth and swallowed big, but he winced and doubled over from an unseen pain.

Raquel whipped her legs off of his lap and threw the blanket to the ground.

"Florence—" Adam started. The name was breathy. It was difficult for him to speak.

"Don't try to talk!" Raquel instructed. She darted for the kitchen behind them, still stealing glances over her shoulder as Adam rubbed the pain in his chest. His eyes were squeezed tight shut. He moaned, the sound as painful and deep as the first night she'd spoken with him out on the porch.

After what felt like an eternity, Raquel found her things. She fumbled through her purse for her cell phone and finally found it tucked into a side pocket. With shaking fingers, she typed in the digits for 9-1-1.

EIGHTEEN

THE AIR CONDITIONING was running high in Adam's lonely wing of the hospital.

Raquel's skin raised in large, prickly goosebumps. The tears that had started on her drive to the hospital darn near froze on her cheeks. The sweat that had pooled under the back of her sports bra and around her neck from the exertion of fighting past her dizziness from earlier and worrying about Adam now left her feeling clammy and too moist.

The cold was making her angry. A kind nurse with a bobbed haircut had asked her if she wanted to stay in Adam's room until his family arrived. Raquel barked at her to talk to someone about the air conditioning. She demanded to know what kind of ignorants ran such a Podunk hospital.

They'd never kicked her out of his room. Instead, Raquel banished herself to the hallway, positively shaking as the cold and anger and frustration finally gave way to what she was really feeling. In the end, the fear and guilt left her shaking far more than the air conditioning. Her bottom lip became raw where she gnawed at it. Her fingers were sore and bleeding where she picked at them from her spot outside Adam's door.

For what felt like the millionth time, the brief thought came to Raquel that she wasn't the type of girl to bark orders at well-meaning nurses or make a scene. But anything had to feel better than this. She would take any distraction she could get.

Grace and her husband, Jack, were the first ones to arrive at the hospital. They found Raquel curled into a ball just outside of Adam's room, her black hair hanging over her face to mask her tears.

The couple exchanged a meaningful look, and Grace squeezed her husband's hand before pushing him away gently towards the doorway to Adam's room.

"Go inside and be with my brother," Grace instructed Jack at the doorway. She kissed his cheek before he nodded and let himself inside.

Grace got down on the ground next to Raquel, tucking her legs up underneath her body. Her dark red hair was tied into a simple knot at the top of her head, and she took out its pins now, letting the waves fall around her shoulders. She ran her fingers through the strands and massaged her scalp like she was enormously tired.

"Poor Adam needs a frequent customer card to this place," Grace mused, her voice dry. "He can't catch a break."

"It's my fault," Raquel muttered.

"It's not your fault," Grace assured her. She put an arm around Raquel's shoulders and pulled her close. The gesture was intended to be comforting, forgiving even. But to Raquel, Grace's arm felt like another load on her back. Another weight just pinning her down.

"Adam had a pulmonary embolism, Grace," Raquel snapped, turning to Adam's sister with a sharp look. "Do you know what that is? It's a blockage in his lung that was caused by a blood clot in his leg. A blood clot that could have been prevented if I had kept him on top of his medications and taking his blood thinners."

Grace sighed again. There was an immense heaviness to her face; for the first time, Raquel noticed that the beautiful young redhead had deep frown lines between her eyes and crow's feet that slashed the sides of her face like wounds.

"This isn't our first rodeo," Grace told Raquel. "Adam has been in and out of this hospital since he was fourteen. Leg repairs, overdoses... my husband Jack was even the one who donated his kidney. We'll get through this. We always do."

Raquel couldn't bear to look Grace in the eyes. "You don't understand." She shook her head. "You're his support system, you're *supposed* to be blindly optimistic..."

"I learned the hard way that sometimes bad things will happen over which you have no control," Grace muttered, perhaps more to herself than to Raquel. "Adam was given a difficult road to walk. But, over time, you'll learn as I have to turn it all over to God and to have faith where you can."

Raquel scoffed. "Look, Grace, I know that you guys are old school Christian cowboys and cowgirls, but can you spare me the Sunday School lesson right now? My boyfriend—" she swallowed hard, forcing herself to self-correct,"—my *patient* has been hospitalized because I was too selfish to do my job."

"Raquel, you are his nurse, not his puppeteer," Grace's brow furrowed. "You can only do your best. You can't force his medications down his throat."

"But I wasn't doing my best, was I?" Raquel could hear her voice raising. People down the hallway were turning to see what the commotion was about. She didn't care. She stood up from the ground, crossing her arms and pacing.

"Adam is in the hospital. He's going through hell because I needed three precious days to kiss and makeup with my best friend."

Grace stood up, too, her bright eyes pleading. "Raquel, you're only human."

"Adam could have died because I chose to watch movies instead of paying attention to the warning signs!" Raquel took a step back. The panicked breathing was beginning to return; she struggled to sustain her words. Headache. Fingers Tingling. Heart beating, heart beating, *heart beating.* "I almost killed him!"

"Okay, calm down," Grace insisted. She stood up, too, her eyes darting around with embarrassment.

"Don't tell me to calm down!" Raquel yelled at her.

The door to Adam's room opened. Jack stood in the doorway, his face concerned. If he could hear her, then Raquel knew that Adam could hear her, too. She could picture him, his usually lush, pink lips still tinged blue. His hair matted down with sweat. His eyes heavy with exhaustion.

She had put him here. She had done this.

New tears were running down Raquel's cheeks before she could stop them. She wiped at them with the back of her shirt sleeve, knowing that her mascara must be streaking down, too.

She was gulping for much-needed air, but she willed herself to stay conscious. Raquel leaned into the pain, let herself feel its full, bright effect for the first time in months. This time, instead of darkening her vision and making her lose focus, it made Raquel's world feel sharper. More dangerous. She needed to know what this felt like. She needed to learn her lesson.

"Adam almost died because I put my feelings before his

health," she announced. "I wasn't a good nurse. I certainly wasn't a good girlfriend."

"Raquel—" Grace started, reaching a hand out. Raquel just kept pacing.

"I was so delusional," she choked on the words, hardly able to speak them aloud. "I thought this was better. I thought *we* were better than I was with Jude. I thought that I had finally gotten things right this time around. That Adam was a good match for me and I was a good match for him. But I was wrong, wasn't I? In the end, there's too much risk in going for someone I want. There's too much danger in falling in love when all that comes of it is disaster."

The clang of metal on tile floor sounded. Raquel gasped as she looked up at the doorway.

There was Adam, IV still attached to his arm. He wasn't as frail and wan as she had thought, but the sight of him in a hospital gown still made her stomach turn.

"You're wrong," he said. His voice was hardly above a whisper. "You can't think that way."

Even now, even as Raquel confessed her most terrifying feelings out loud, she still wanted him. She felt that pull to Adam, the undeniable desire to nurse him and comfort him and help him in any way that she could. Raquel stumbled back, scared of her own longing. She bumped into someone standing behind her. She whipped around.

"Raquel, thank you so much for calling on your way to the hospital." Esther Gardner gave Raquel a grim smile, oblivious to the chaos she had just walked in on. Adam's father, Samuel, stood just behind her holding a small bag of Adam's toiletries. Behind them stood the rest of his siblings.

The familiar wave of dark dizziness rolled across Raquel's vision. She stumbled back in the opposite direction, nearly tripping on Grace who had walked forward.

Raquel felt trapped, pinned. Her breathing was quickening as it had before.

"Raquel, just come in and talk." Her head twisted around at the sound of Adam's voice. He had stepped out of the doorway, his face contorted with worry and pain. He reached a hand out to her and winced at the effort.

"No..." Raquel slipped past Grace and backed down the hall. "I can't do this..."

Before she knew what was happening, Raquel found herself flying down the hospital halls. Between the tears and the impending panic attack, her vision was getting worse and she had to narrowly dodge doctors and nurses who tried to stop her and ask what was wrong. She ran and ran and ran, relying only the sounds of her tennis shoes slapping against the tile as a reminder of where she was and where she needed to be.

When Raquel finally burst through the hospital double doors, she bent forward, gulping down fresh air like she had just come up from drowning.

It was brighter outside than she had expected. It was a hot, summer day, complete with a Western sun that beat the grass of the hospital lawn into curving, dry submission. Raquel shielded her eyes against the brightness, but she turned her face to the sky to let the sun erase some of her tears.

She opened her eyes at the sharp *caw* of a bird flying overhead. It looked like a turkey vulture, one of the desert creatures that Adam had pointed out to her during one of their walks around his little house. It eyeballed the hospital grounds, scanning for dead things.

Raquel's gaze shifted out to the distance, where she could just see the low-rising buildings of Main Street. They shimmered in the sun, a wavy mirage. So lonely. So old.

How could Raquel have ever thought she could make a home out here in Goldfinch? Everything about this desert was so hostile. It took far more than it gave back. And if she dared to stay any longer, maybe it would take her, too. It would crumble her up into an oblivion of unrequited desires or ill-fated romance or unreasonable expectations.

She needed to go home. She needed to get far, far away from this godforsaken place.

Back in the freezing air conditioning of the hospital, Raquel had regretted her usual sports bra and yoga pants attire. It had been too exposing, too cold. Now, though, she sent up a silent thank you for her choice of clothing. She took off at a brisk pace, heading back to Adam's home to repack her duffel bags.

NINETEEN

"I'M SORRY, love. We just closed. I can wrap you up some takeout if you can wait just a mo—"

Ida stopped mopping her restaurant floor to look up at the door. Raquel stood under the still-tinkling bell, bags hooked over each shoulder. Her cheeks had been blackened by running mascara.

"I have to admit," Ida started, voice low and cautious. "I'm not sure I know the right order for you today, love."

"I'm not here for food." Raquel hung her head, having to concentrate hard not to break down in tears again. "I just left the Gardners my letter of resignation. I'm here to say goodbye."

Ida put the mop back in its bucket and stepped, ignoring her wet floor, to go to Raquel. She hugged her tight, squishing the girl's face to her massive bosom.

"What happened today?" Ida asked, face contorted with concern. "What brought this on?"

"I let him get hurt." Raquel hung her head. "Adam's in the hospital because I let myself fall for him and get distracted. It only further proves that bad things happen when I let my guard down."

"You're not really leaving?"

"I have to," Raquel reiterated. "Coming here was a stupid idea. Taking this job, being his nurse—"

"And loving Adam?" Ida supplied, pulling Raquel back to look at her.

"No," Raquel shook her head. "I'm not saying that out loud. It's a bad idea. The last time that I went all in with someone I would up with my heart broken. At some point, I have to finally learn to protect myself."

"Oh, sweetheart," Ida pulled her close again. "Spoken like someone who has never truly loved before."

"I loved Jude," Raquel insisted, pushing back. She wiped at her eyes with the back of her sleeve. "We spent *years* together. I was so wrecked by our breakup that I cut off my best friend and moved to a different state. I know what I'm talking about."

Ida cocked her head, studying Raquel closely. "I'm sorry, is Adam the same person as Jude?"

"You know he's not," Raquel admitted. "That's probably what attracted me to him in the first place. Typical broken-hearted city girl, falling for the rancher who represents a new life and a fresh start..."

Ida was quiet for a long time. She let Raquel step away from her arms, and she took a seat at one of her freshly-cleaned tables. After a minute, she pulled her apron up over her head, folded it, and set it in front of her. She looked up at Raquel.

"Did you know some of the bitties in town have a nickname for me?" She asked Raquel.

Raquel shook her head. Ida sighed and continued. "'I-do

Ida.' Thought they were *real* clever because I've been married four times."

A reluctant smile curved Raquel's lips slightly. "It *is* a pretty good name."

"Alright, it is." Ida grinned back. "Honestly, love, I kinda like the nickname. It suits me. I love love. It's even my most overused term of endearment. I love the falling for the hunky guy, the steamy Western nights in the tall grass, the proposal. All of it. And four different times, my marriages have ended in terrible, bitter divorce."

"Why do you keep coming back to love?" Raquel asked, her voice low. "Aren't you terrified of going through those breakups again?"

"Of course, I'm scared," Ida admitted. It was hard for Raquel to think of Ida being scared of anything, with the way her large, commanding presence took up room even in the quiet, lonely restaurant. "But the reward—no matter how brief—sure outweighs the risk, don't it?"

A quiet settled between the women. A million thoughts rushed up to the front of Raquel's brain at once. But despite Ida's comforting words, she still felt that lingering sense of anxiety. Ida had had decades to practice falling in and out of love. To refine how she put herself out there for others and let them past her walls.

Raquel... well, she just wasn't like that. Maybe she was in the Great Before, back when she'd been so sure of herself and her relationships and her friendships. Now, she was just the timid nurse who had trouble asking for a promotion. The girl who got panic attacks in the grocery story because she couldn't even choose between ice cream flavors.

She was the girl who hadn't been able to say "I love you" back to Adam Gardner, even when he'd been brave enough to say it first.

Raquel squeezed Ida's hand, but kept her eyes trained on the ground.

"I'm sorry," she said. "I think I just need to go home for a while."

Ida nodded. With one soft hand, she tilted Raquel's chin up, forcing her to look at her. "I'll keep a cinnamon roll set aside for you every day if you decide to come back."

Raquel nodded and smiled the tiniest amount. She didn't have the right words to say. She hooked her bags over her arms again and headed across the wet floor to the exit. Her dusty shoes would surely leave tracks on the fresh wash —she hoped that Ida would forgive her, but she didn't have the wherewithal to turn back and apologize.

It was back to the bus station, where this nightmare had all started.

TWENTY

ONE WEEK LATER

UGH. Didn't television stations play *anything* but *Full House* reruns on Saturday mornings? Raquel passed two channels running it while she was flipping, angrily muttering under her breath each time until Abby snatched the remote for herself.

"How about a movie?" Abby suggested. She passed Raquel the popcorn as she got up from the couch to rifle through the various DVDs of the Villanueva collection. It was seven o'clock in the morning. Raquel didn't care; she scooped up a massive handful of buttery goodness and passed it back.

They'd been at it all night. Abby was the first person that Raquel called when her phone finally got service, and the first person to show up to welcome her back to Vegas. She'd been by her side nearly every other night since. The week had dragged on, made worse by how much Raquel's mother hadn't been thrilled—Miriam still didn't trust Abby, a fact which was made clear by her near-constant presence throughout the night.

"You could go on a date with another man," Miriam suggested as she floated through the living room with a hamper full of clean laundry. "Or perhaps there's some lovely girl whose boyfriend you could steal. That might make you feel better."

"*Mama*, hush." Raquel shot her mother a look, and Miriam put one hand up in defeat.

She'd come around eventually. Abby had been a permanent fixture of Raquel's life since they met back in kindergarten. It was hard to erase so much history, even if there was a hiccup in their story.

"Sorry," Abby whispered with a wince as Miriam finally left the room. She'd apologized every time Raquel's mother made a comment. She settled onto the couch next to Raquel as the pre-movie trailers began to roll.

"Don't be," Raquel reached out and took her friend's hand. "I'm happy you're here."

Abby pulled an old quilt up over her legs and sat in silence for a moment, staring straight forward. She cleared her throat. "Is your mom right?"

"Right about what?" Raquel cocked her head.

"Do you ever feel afraid... that I'd come for your boyfriend again? Can a person ever really forgive and forget something like that?" Abby pulled her hand back to intertwine her fingers together. She still stared dead ahead.

"What boyfriend?" Raquel rolled her eyes and sighed. Better to keep the unreasonably worries she'd felt back at the ranch to herself, especially now that her time with Adam was in the past. She slunk further into the depths of the couch cushions. "I got rid of that last one pretty much all on my own, thank you very much."

A trailer for a new rom-com started up. A sassy, confident leading lady exchanged witty banter with some Freddie Prinze Jr. lookalike. Raquel's stomach turned. He wasn't Adam, but he was close enough. "Can we fast forward through these things?" she asked Abby.

Abby pressed pause and set the remote down. She turned to Raquel, searching her eyes. "Seriously," she started again. "Do you think this is 100%? We're built to last, through boys or fights or other drama? Am I just hurting you by making you fight for our friendship?"

"Abby." Raquel forced her friend to give up her hands once more. She squeezed Abby's fingers and smiled. "It's 100%. I was scared for a while that we wouldn't make it. But in the end, coming back to you and taking the chance that I could get hurt all over again is worth the risk. I want you in my life."

Her stomach took an unexpected dip. *Taking the chance that I could get hurt all over again is worth the risk. I want you in my life.*

The irony wasn't lost on her. Raquel knew that it was quite the feat to work up the courage to keep her best friend in her life, but she was still too terrified to fight for the man she clearly loved.

Thinking too much about Adam again made her want to curl under the quilt and die.

"Let's just get back to the movie." She smiled and gave Abby's hand one final squeeze. The last trailer faded to black and the girls' movie started up.

Raquel recognized these opening credits. She'd seen this movie in theaters. *Pitch Black.* A thrilling, improbable, and kind of cheesy sci-fi flick. One of Raquel's modern favorites. Classic Abby choice.

It would have been someone else's movie choice, too.

Raquel bolted up from her spot on the couch and pressed "open" on the DVD player without bothering to stop the movie.

"Everything okay?" Abby asked, puzzled.

"How about something else?" Raquel said. "I don't know if I'm in the mood for something so dramatic and action-packed. Maybe no sci-fi at all."

Abby scooted to the edge of the couch and clicked off the TV. "Honestly, I'm not sure I'm really in a movie mood anyway. I just suggested watching one to help distract you. But we can try something else?"

"Something else," Raquel agreed, nodding.

"We can head down to the Strip," Abby suggested. "Tina Brycroft is working Caesars Palace tonight. We can say hi and then hit up a few tables. Nothing like losing all your hard-earned cash to make you forget about other miseries."

Raquel had stopped listening after Abby's first sentence. She was already mentally far away, seated at another card table across from Adam Gardner. Watching him push back a flyaway lock of hair as he considered his next move. Feeling the sweat collect on the back of her neck and knowing that it wasn't just because they were playing reverse-strip-blackjack.

"How about a walk outside?" Raquel blurted out. "We've been in here all night and I think I'm starting to go stir-crazy. We can just walk the neighborhood. Get some fresh air."

Abby nodded. "Course."

The girls found their shoes in the foyer and pulled open the front door. Raquel winced as they stepped out in the morning sun. The world shouldn't be allowed to feel so dang bright and glorious when she felt so miserable.

Couldn't Vegas rain for once? Even a dust storm would do the trick.

Abby's phone went off as they rounded out of the front yard and headed toward the main road. She pulled it discreetly from her pocket, eyeballing the tiny screen.

"Jude?" Raquel asked. It still felt so odd to ask that of Abby. And yet, for the first time in a very long time, saying his name out loud didn't set off her breathing. It didn't leave her feeling dizzy and panicked and embarrassed.

"I'm sorry," Abby apologized. "He's been trying to get through all night. I'm sure he's just wondering when I'll be home. I'll call him back later."

"Thanks," Raquel muttered. She shoved her hands into her sweatpant pockets as she walked. Together, the girls headed up a steep hill, letting the silence settle in.

It was too loud here, Raquel thought to herself. How had she never noticed before how loud the city was? She could hear the freeway traffic from where they walked. A neighbor's dog whined loud and long. A trash can rumbled in the distance as the garbage truck made its rounds.

She missed the rooster. Who would have guessed?

Raquel smiled to herself as she thought about what Adam might think of that. Florence, the city girl, finally appreciating even the small annoyances of ranch life.

Maybe she more than appreciated it. Maybe she outright missed it. Raquel could still picture that perfect, peaceful morning when they'd taken their first walk together around Adam's property. He'd looked so beautiful in the Arizona sunshine. His blonde hair was near-translucent in the morning rays. His smile had glistened when he spoke. And the robe he had worn had flapped open and loose, exposing a strong, tanned farmer's chest.

More than the way he looked, Raquel missed the way

she felt with him that day. Their easy conversation. The common ground she hadn't expected to find with him when they both realized they were the objects of unwanted pity. The friendship they had formed on snark and insults and misery.

The girls took one last turn, and completed the square around the Villanueva's small neighborhood. Abby had her phone out; she was absorbed with typing up some message. Raquel didn't mind. She let the forbidden thoughts run through her mind freely now, let herself get lost in the ache of nostalgia.

Had she made a mistake in leaving Adam behind? Was there some small chance that he, like Abby, was worth a little risk?

Raquel didn't want to feel this way anymore. She was tired of the sadness and the anxiety and the constant second-guessing all of her decisions. Couldn't she—for once —just know what she wanted *and* have the guts to reach out and take it?

Suddenly, Raquel found herself aching to return to the couch with the quilt. She wanted to pull it right over her head and not come out for another decade. Surely, things would be better by then, right? She could have forgotten about Adam and about Goldfinch and about—

"Hey."

She stopped short of her home's doorway, her whole body going tight.

Jude had his hands buried deep in his pockets. His head hung low. He'd changed his hair since Raquel had seen him last. He still looked very much like a Josh Hartnett clone, but a little more clean cut and younger. He had the same familiar, charming gap-toothed smile. It showed itself now, as he looked to Raquel with the strangest mix of embarrassment and hope. He even smelled the same, like casino smoke and sweet cologne.

Raquel sighed and squeezed her eyes closed for a moment, working up the nerve to cross all the way over to him. Couldn't she just catch a break for once?

TWENTY-ONE

JUDE SHUFFLED, kicking at a rock that had rolled in front of the doorway.

"Sorry we had to meet this way," he mumbled. "I didn't... it's just... well, I didn't exactly want to knock and face your mom. She's terrifying when she takes off that flip-flop to hit you with it."

Abby flicked him on the shoulder. "I told you we were fine," she chided. "You shouldn't have come out here."

"You weren't taking my calls," he told her, one hand going up to grip her elbow. "It's been over a day. What about—"

"Work?" Abby supplied. "I called in. Gavin was fine with trading my shift, don't worry. Did you—"

"Yeah, I picked up Mrs. Runyan's mail."

"And you—"

"Returned our movies to Blockbuster. I picked up *Beetlejuice* for this weekend."

"Perfect." Abby grinned.

Raquel cleared her throat, and they both jumped. It was

like they had forgotten she was there. The awkwardness and nerves immediately returned to Jude's face.

"Have you guys always done this?" She asked them.

The question took both Abby and Jude off guard.

"Done what?" Abby asked.

"The finishing each other's sentences routine. The lighting up when you see one another." Raquel's brow knit tight in the middle of her forehead.

"Um..." Jude started, looking just as pained as he had that first day when they'd sat Raquel down on the living room couch to tell her their news.

"Kind of," Abby admitted. Jude and Abby glanced at one another, a brief, flickering expression that Raquel suddenly felt sure she had seen before.

And just like that, it was like that tiny intimacy between them unlocked something in Raquel. More memories rushed to the surface of her brain, looking somehow different than the way she'd spent the last four months of her life recalling them.

She saw herself spending weekends at the mall with Abby and Jude, laughing when the pair of them ordered the exact same meal in the food court. She remembered heading to bed early after a late night spent talking with her best friends, half-listening from her room as they stayed up late to play another round of *Final Fantasy* on the PlayStation. She recalled Christmases where Abby and Jude knew just what to give each other, vacations where the trio fell asleep on the couch together.

Opposites attract, Raquel had reminded herself over and over again when Abby and Jude had more in common than herself and her boyfriend. And they did sometimes, that was true. But in this instance, Raquel's insistence that she and Jude had been perfect for one another had turned out to be the biggest cause for her heartache; she hadn't been able to see that there was someone better for him, and that he, in turn, was meant for someone else.

And meanwhile, there was a man in a hospital room back in Goldfinch, Arizona. Someone who had connected with Raquel instantly, even when they were bickering back and forth over whether or not he needed a live-in nurse. Someone who never looked anywhere but at her. Who fought to make her feel at home and made her—for the first time in so many long, painful months—even begin to consider taking the risk of putting her heart on the line once more.

The front door creaked open, causing the trio to jump back in surprise.

"Do not shoot!" Diego teased as he rolled his chair up to the entry. "I am not my daughter ready to beat you with her Chancla."

See? Jude mouthed to the girls and gestured at Raquel's abuelo.

Diego raised one eyebrow and half-smiled. "Do not think you are off the hook yet though, amigo. I just came to check on my baby girl when I heard voices outside. I may only have one leg, but I can still beat the trash out of you if you try anything funny."

Jude's ears turned bright red and threw up his hands, hurriedly nodding. "Yes, sir."

"We were just leaving, Mr. Villanueva," Abby explained. She put a hand to Jude's arm and nodded her head in the direction of the main road. "Better get going."

The couple started off to where Jude had parked his car. Diego lingered in the doorway, watching with crossed arms and pursed lips as they left.

Raquel turned to him as the car started in the distance.

"One leg, but you can still kick his butt, huh?" She smiled wryly.

Diego's tough exterior melted into a mischievous grin. "I have to maintain my street credibility, Mija."

"I think by calling it 'street credibility' instead of just 'street cred' you may be already fighting a losing battle on that front." She grinned.

Diego scoffed and turned his chair to head back inside. "Come in, it is boiling outside."

Raquel followed him back into the house. Catching sight of the quilt-laden couch and half-empty snack bowls instantly reminded her of what she'd gone outside to leave behind. She paused for just a moment too long, hovering in the foyer.

Diego noticed. He rolled around to face Raquel, crossing his arms as he had when he sized up Jude. "When was the last time we had a grandfatherly chat, Mija?"

"Hmm, was that back when you were afraid to talk to me about the birds and the bees or when you gave me the pamphlet on my changing body?" She extended him a small smile. "I'm almost thirty, not thirteen."

"Very funny." Diego smirked. He rolled closer and took her hand.

"I'm afraid that my problems have grown to be a lot more complex anyway." Raquel sighed and hung her head.

"I will admit that I listened in at the door a little," Diego said. "I heard you talking with Jude and Abby. And Ida has told me all the rest."

"You two talk without me now?" Raquel asked.

"Mija, I do not understand," he squeezed her hand, his eyes imploring her own. "You care for this boy. He cares for you. You seem at peace with Abby and Jude now. What is stopping you from returning to Adam?"

"It's not that easy." Raquel fumbled for the right words. "I know I want him. And now I'm sure that we're a better match than Jude and I ever were. That's not the hard part anymore. It's putting myself out there. Risking my heart and all the panic I've felt for months now. Is the reward ever worth all that risk?"

Diego was quiet for a minute, his eyes seeming to study out the intricacies of the foyer tile. He sighed before he opened his mouth to speak again. "I trained for years to become the best pilot I could be. When I was little, I got books from the library about Charles Lindbergh and Amelia Earheart. I slept with a plastic plane that my mama got from the thrift shop until I was eight."

Raquel laughed at that. The little plane was still on display in her abuleo's room, propped up next to his medals. Diego smiled, too.

"I never could have known that my career would end in a plane crash," he said. "That I would lose my leg. I could not walk, much less fly."

A lump formed in Raquel's throat as he spoke. She had never heard her grandfather speak so openly about his accident. He had mentioned it plenty of times in passing, but always with a hint of snark or sarcasm. This felt different. Raw. Vulnerable.

"For all I knew, I could receive the Medal of Honor one day," Diego's smile was soft and nostalgic. "The end was never my ultimate consideration. The real reward was in the journey. I fell in love with the blue sky and the white clouds, and I would trade my last good leg to do it all again. I'm grateful I tried to fly. It was my greatest privilege."

Tears were stinging at the corners of Raquel's eyes. She didn't want to break down in front of her abuelo, but as he squeezed her fingers again she felt them beginning to roll.

A garbled sound escaped her lips as she tried to find the right words. Adam was her own passage into the sky. He took her higher than she'd ever been before. And, unlike Diego, she had two good legs that she now knew she might give up forever to get him back.

"Abuelo, I'm scared." As soon as Raquel said the words, she better understood the cause of her anxieties, her panic attacks, and her newfound sense of general uncertainty. She *was* scared.

Diego shrugged and smiled. "I get that."

"Adam could fire me for sending him to the hospital. He could yell at me for being selfish and petty. He could not say anything at all, just ice me out." She sighed and hung her head. "That might be worst of all."

"He could do those things," Diego acknowledged.

"No sage advice to get rid of the fear, huh? She asked him, still holding out a little hope that he might present her with a magical cure-all.

"We all get scared," he told her. "But instead of being so terrified of what could go wrong, why not choose to get excited about what could go right?"

Deep-seated instinct told Raquel to keep pushing back, to keep resisting his guidance. But she was sure running out of excuses.

She settled for rolling her eyes and smiling at him. "I hate that you're so good at this."

"I'm your abuelo. It is a sort of job requirement." He grinned.

A noise sounded from the hallway, and Diego and Raquel both looked up.

"Your mama must be done in her bedroom," Diego commented. "Careful not to tell her that boy was here, or she might use the Chancla on *you*."

Raquel laughed at that, the sound happier and lighter than she could have anticipated.

Diego reached up, his thumb tracing the gentle curve of her jaw. "Go pack your bags again, Mija. Go do it now. I have already made arrangements for you to get back to Goldfinch."

"Abuelo..." Raquel's mouth dropped open as Diego fumbled in his pocket and produced a bus ticket.

"You can stay with our friend Ida," he told her, placing the ticket into her open hand. "We have made all the arrangements. Just in case you changed your mind."

"Abuelo, I—"

"Choose to be excited," he reminded her. "Choose to be loved."

Raquel's heartbeat was so loud, she could hear it in her ears. She nodded, near-numb, still not knowing quite what to say back to him. "Thank you," she mustered up.

Diego smiled and pulled her face down to his. He planted a kiss on her cheek and hugged her close. "What is it those country boys say? Ah! Go on, git."

Raquel laughed. "I think... there's one more stop I have to make before I go."

Diego nodded. "You do what you need to do. And be sure to call me when you get to Ida."

"I will," she agreed, giving his hand one final squeeze.

Raquel started off to her room, already mentally sorting through what she might need to pack. She stopped short as she felt her abuelo's hand on her arm once more.

"Oh, and Mija," he added. His eyes were looking anywhere but hers, the definition of inconspicuous. "Do you happen to know if our friend Ida is seeing anyone? I just want to be sure that there aren't any strange men that will be staying with you in Goldfinch..."

Raquel brayed with laughter, near doubling over. For the second time that morning, it struck her how farcical it was that she hadn't been able to see a love connection earlier. Ida and Diego had spent all that time on the phone together, talking about God knows what when they weren't discussing Raquel. 'I-do Ida' might have just struck again.

She grinned and shook her head as she left her grandfather to head back to her bedroom. Here he was, taking a risk again. And Raquel couldn't be happier for him.

TWENTY-TWO

TINA BRYCROFT WAS a sight to behold in her toga-themed mini dress. She gave a little twirl as she strutted and showed off for Raquel, getting a few wolf-whistles from already-drunk gamblers. Tina waggled her fingers in their direction, smiling as she loudly *popped* a fat pink bubble of gum.

"Uniform here does wonders," Tina explained to Raquel with a knowing look. "If you're really looking for good money, you should apply at Caesars. Sometimes I don't even have to really serve, I just flirt around and get tips."

Raquel felt the curves of her ears burning as another group of middle-aged men tried to flag down Tina. Tina blew them a kiss, sending them howling and waving cash in her direction.

"Erm, no," Raquel said as Tina returned, tucking a few bills and chips into her bra. "That would... take longer than I need. I'm looking for fast cash."

"This is Vegas, baby," Tiny grinned. "It's all fast cash, if you're lucky."

"I'm just in need of a little guidance," Raquel explained.

"It's not, um, an *Ocean's Eleven* plan or anything. But can you help anyway?"

Tina rolled her head back and huffed. "Ugh, you're no fun," she complained. Nevertheless, she put a hand to Raquel's back and turned her toward the casino floor. "Try the blackjack table first. Winners always come out of there. Craps is probably a good second, since your odds are 50/50. But you've got a cute body, Raquel. If you feel like snagging one of our uniforms and giving it a go, I'll keep things hush for you..."

"*No*," Raquel emphasized, feeling the blush fully takeover the rest of her face. "Blackjack it is," she said. "Thank you, Tina."

Tina shrugged and headed back over to the group of disorderly tourists. Raquel took a deep breath and stood at the edge of the casino floor, holding her purse close to her body as she sized up the blackjack table.

There would be no more panic attacks. No more talking herself out of taking what she wanted. She knew how to play. And, more importantly, she knew what she was playing for.

Raquel pulled out her phone and flipped it open. No missed calls. She'd been trying the Gardner Ranch all day, calling Adam's house and his parents' all to the rejection of busy signals. Had he blocked her number? Kept the phone off the hook? The thought of Adam's having grown tired of waiting on her to come around made Raquel feel less sure of herself. The fears were returning, despite her abuelo's continued assurances. Raquel almost flagged down Tina again to tell her she had changed her mind.

Almost.

Instead, Raquel gulped as she walked over to the table and sat down next to a couple with Midwestern accents and

Hawaiian shirts. She pulled out the cash that Tina had helped her to procure when she got to Caesars Palace and set her first bet on the table. The couples' eyes went wide.

"Gee, you got one of them gamblin' addictions?" The man asked her, leaning in close like that might convince Raquel to confide in him.

"Harold..." His wife winced and tugged on his sleeve, her wrist wimpy and bent.

"No," Raquel laughed. Or, at the very least, she tried to. The sound came out breathy and unsustained.

"Which denomination would you like?" The dealer asked her, taking her cash.

"Give me the purples. Please?" Raquel tacked on the polite request at the last second, still second-guessing her plan more than she'd like. She gulped.

The dealer slid over her chips and Raquel picked them up. She dropped the majority in her purse, but saved one for the table. She ran a fingertip over the shiny purple chip just before she set it down. Five hundred dollars. Harold was right: it was gambling addiction kind of money.

It was also darn near every penny that she'd saved working for Adam Gardner. The money he had gotten from raising Buck Johnson's fillies, recycled back into Raquel's grand gesture for their relationship. Five hundred on the table, and every other cent she'd earned stored away in the safety of her purse.

The game began.

Raquel's first hand went over easy. She felt a new wave of dizziness as her winnings were returned to her. Lord—was her plan really working? Slow and steady and she could pull this off. She could get the money she needed and return to Goldfinch. Maybe—just maybe—it would be enough to earn her Adam's forgiveness for running off. For leaving him broken and alone in a hospital.

For making him feel something, but being too terrified to allow herself to feel the same things in return.

The game began again. She felt more confident, more sure. She grinned, despite her efforts to stay cool and collected. Perhaps this could be like one of those movies. She'd remember those blackjack skills that she honed playing with Adam, and win exactly the amount she needed and...

... But Raquel's hand wasn't as good this time around. She had an eleven against the dealer's strong ten. She stiffened her back, suddenly relating to Adam's impulse to hide his cards when they first played back at his house. Raquel smiled at the memory. She strengthened her resolve.

"Hit me," she ordered, doubling down.

"Bust," the dealer told her in return, sliding Raquel's chips to the dealer side of the table in one swift motion.

Raquel's heart beat faster; her stomach clenched. Okay, so maybe not like in the movies. But this could just be a little hiccup. She'd try again; gotta have faith. She dug into her purse and held her breath as she placed another shiny purple chip down in front of her.

"Going again?" Harold asked, as he and his anxious wife abandoned their spots and drinks to come stand behind her and watch her play. "You bettin' the farm, kid?"

"Something like that," she admitted. The dealer started the next round, the one that only she was playing. Her stomach was in knots. She couldn't count cards, or bribe the dealer, or any of the other things that gamblers sometimes did to make an easy buck. All she could do was play and hope for the best.

The sweat on the back of her neck picked up. Once

again, Raquel's mind flashed away to that other game of blackjack, in which she wore a heavy coat. A knit winter hat. A game in which she'd also been distracted thinking about Adam Gardner, and how much she wanted him.

"I'm sorry," the dealer announced, sliding her chips away once more.

Raquel blew out some of the tight air in her chest through a tiny hole between her lips. Harold ordered drinks for the table while his wife fretted about whether they'd brought enough cash in their fanny packs.

"This one's on me," he told Raquel. He patted her on the back, a touch laden with far more pity than the flirtatious gestures she'd seen directed at Tina earlier. The interaction only made Raquel feel more anxious. She hadn't brought *that* much cash, and she was quickly blowing through what she had. What if she failed at this? What if she wasted all her summer money and had no grand gesture to bring back to Gardner Ranch to win over Adam?

"Go again," she told the dealer, sliding back more chips. Her purse was getting ever lighter. Her heart was beating harder.

Raquel won the next hand, but her victory was short-lived. She was on a losing streak, and Harold the Tourist kicked up a cheering squad in her honor, his wife still weakly pulling at his sleeve like she was embarrassed of the spectacle. Soon there was a small crowd around the table, all of them saying prayers aloud that Raquel wouldn't blow through the rest of her cash.

But Raquel hardly noticed. She was zeroed in. Focused. Trying not to think of anything but the cards and Adam and how badly she needed this.

"Bust," the dealer announced again, pulling back her latest offering of chips.

Raquel stuck her hand back in her purse. It was empty. She collapsed back in her chair, running her hands through her hair. What could she possibly do now?

Her breathing was quickening as it always did these days, but she fought to maintain her composure. She wasn't going to give in to the anxiety this time. She was going to find another way to come out of this on top.

"Come on, girlie, you're gonna turn out to be the new Edward Thorpe! I can feel it!" Harold announced, clapping her back. "How much are you betting next, firecracker? Five hundo? Six hundo?"

"No more hundos," Raquel muttered, sitting back up and waving the dealer off. She turned in her chair as the crowd behind her groaned. "I... I've actually blown through everything I brought with me."

The onlookers shrugged and started to head off in their separate directions, but Harold gestured for Raquel to leave her spot at the table and come sit by him and his wife at a nearby bar. Raquel did as she was told, trudging across the dirty casino floor to sit on a cracked pleather stool. She let loose a massive sigh as she sat down, burying her face in her hands.

"That was really somethin', kiddo." Harold grinned. "Do we get the story now? You gonna tell us what all the show was about?"

"Harold..." His wife was tugging at his sleeve again, reminding him not to be nosy. But even she looked interested, sitting on the edge of her seat and leaning in to see if Raquel chose to engage, her arched eyebrows nearly disappearing into her hairline.

Raquel grappled for the right words, but her now-familiar timidity was trickling back. She couldn't believe that she hadn't won.

"I don't know what I expected." Raquel finally muttered, looking back up. "There's a boy back in Arizona. I was trying to earn the money to help him start his own corral."

Harold's eyes went wide. "Vegas ain't the route most philanthropists traditionally take."

"It wasn't philanthropy so much as a bargaining chip to gain his forgiveness," Raquel explained. She sounded pathetic, even to herself. "I messed up with him. I think he might have been the love of my life, and I ran away. I can't go back to him empty handed. I mean, I could, but it wouldn't feel right."

"Ah, so this was your grand gesture." Harold nodded knowingly.

"Something like that," Raquel agreed. "I want to prove that I'll fight for him, that I'll take risks and put myself out there and shoot for love even if the stakes are high."

Harold's wife made a small noise like a mouse squeaking. She put a hand to her heart, her brows knitting together.

Harold crossed his arms and sighed. "Lucky for you, kiddo, Vegas is good for more than just winning money. Caesar's makes an Old Fashioned that'll knock your socks off."

"Harold?" His wife was tugging on his sleeve again.

"This drink's on us," Harold continued. "No one lonely should drink alone."

"Harold..." His wife tried again.

"Sorry, sweetheart, yes?" Harold turned to his wife, slipping an arm around her waist.

She tugged at her fanny pack and unzipped it, producing several purple chips of her own. She handed them to her husband, gesturing for him to pass them along to Raquel.

"We own a car dealership back in Minnesota," she explained with a quick shrug. Her thin pink lips pulled out of their tight line and into something that vaguely resembled a smile as Raquel took the chips, her brow furrowed as she tried to understand. "We had a good year and we're here for vacation. We don't need the cash. But you—" The wife's eyes flicked back to Harold, and her smile transformed into something more full, more fleshed out. "—You need help getting back to your Harold. And we can help with that."

Harold's wife gave his arm a quick squeeze instead of pulling on his sleeve.

Raquel shook her head. "I couldn't possibly take this," she argued. "There's got to be several thousand more than what I came in with..."

"My Harold is a very good gambler," his wife said, nodding.

Harold's chest puffed with pride, and he grinned. "What can I say? People hear the accent and think all I know is corn or Budweiser."

"Take the money," his wife insisted. "And go!"

"I'm not sure what to say." Raquel shook her head. "Thank you doesn't seem to cut it."

Tina Brycroft passed by the bar as Raquel tucked the purple chips into her bag. Her eyes went wide, and she sidled up next to the group's stools.

"Raquel, were you a big winner tonight? I think drinks might be on you when my shift is over." Tina's eyes sparkled as she surveyed their gathering. Her gaze landed on Harold, and she hipped her way over to him, a sly smile on her face. "You a big winner too, darlin'?"

Harold's wife turned pink in the cheeks. She tugged on his sleeve once more, urgent as ever. "Harold..."

TWENTY-THREE

GOLDFINCH LOOKED the same as it ever had.

When Raquel's bus had rolled into town just after 2 a.m., it had been too dark and she had been too tired to take in the sights. Ida had been waiting at the station, a boxed-up cinnamon roll in hand and a smile on her face, to welcome Raquel to her small apartment just behind the restaurant. They'd walked over, Raquel had taken the quick tour, and then she collapsed into bed with her clothes still on and the little purse of Harold's cash still strapped over her arm. Her last memories had been of Ida murmuring on the phone to her abuelo, before she finally gave in to stressful dreams of rocky road ice cream and twinkling Christmas lights.

In the light of the cool morning, though, Raquel had been able to take it all in. The dreams were already fading, and so was the last of the apprehension she had brought into town with her. She was ready. She'd eaten the cold remnants of last night's cinnamon roll as she walked Main Street, thinking about what she planned to do and say when she saw Adam.

How could Raquel have ever thought of this place as

hostile? How could she have ever thought of Goldfinch as anything but her adopted home?

The nature sang to her. The rising sun speared through the branches of saguaro cacti, lighting the plains and sparse vegetation as though they were on fire. The barest hints of dew still sparkled on thorns and grasses, eager to give in quickly to the burn of a new day. Small rodents scampered just beyond Raquel's feet on the path to the Gardner Ranch. She smiled as she heard the faint crow of a familiar, persistent rooster. She tucked the trash from her makeshift breakfast into her purse as the Gardner property came into view.

The main house was large and grand. It rose up from the land like it had been there since before the rest of the town, at peace with an existence that was all its own. Its fields rolled. Its animals were quiet and calm. Gardner Ranch was undeniably beautiful.

But it was hard for Raquel to take notice of anything more than Adam's little house beyond the hill. She trekked through the fields up to the home, keeping her eyeline focused on its front door. She could not be dissuaded now.

At long last, she reached the house's steps. She marched up to them and held her hand up to knock. She paused just before her fist made contact with the wood—Adam was already opening the front door.

"Raquel?"

She stumbled down a step, surprised by his answering before she could knock. All the words she had prepared seemed to escape her.

Adam didn't look as wan as he had in the hospital. His complexion was bright and healthy once more. He stood straight and tall. He wore the same stupid fluffy white robe that he had the day she'd found him watching *Full House*, and it gaped open to reveal an equally healthy-looking stretch of chest and muscle.

"You... you didn't take my calls," Raquel stammered, finally finding her voice. "So I.... um... I...."

She shoved forward her little purse, forcing Adam to take it. He looked at her confused for a moment, and she gestured for him to open it.

"It's not much, but it's a start," Raquel told him. As she started talking, the words she had rehearsed over and over again on the walk over finally began to supply themselves. "It's enough to start in on set up for your own corral on your parents' property. If you want to."

"Raquel." Adam's brow furrowed in between his bright blue eyes, contorting his face with emotion. "You don't have to give me all this—"

"It's not a gift," Raquel blurted out, clarifying. "It's a loan." She cleared her throat and took the step back up the stairs. Closer to Adam.

"And if I'm being honest," she continued. *Deep breath.* "It's more for me than it is for you. I need to put roots down and I'm starting with this corral. For once, I need to push back my fears and go after what I want. And what I want is *you*, Adam Gardner. I want your horses and your sarcasm and your terrible sci-fi movies and blackjack games and that small square of frontier that you told me you wanted for yourself. So it's a loan, because you're not getting rid of me anytime soon. I've finally decided to find what I want in this world and to take it. And that's you."

As Raquel finally stopped talking, Adam looked like he might say something in return. He stepped toward her, his lush pink mouth just opening. Raquel felt a spear of the old insecurity stabbing through her, so she plowed on with the act she had rehearsed and pushed past him into his house.

"Come on in," he said with a small laugh, trailing her inside.

Raquel turned back to him, the words ready to tumble out of her mouth before they could fully arrive in her brain.

"If there are any Cheetos in the house, I eat them all. You know what, scratch that: if there are any snacks in the house, consider them gone. It made Jude and Abby crazy. They could never bring any good food back to my place."

Adam looked puzzled, but intrigued. "I'm sorry?" He asked her. "Raquel, just sit down for a second—"

But she headed toward the hallway, ignoring his interjections. Her heart was racing. "I can't be trusted with an iron, so if you need something done, you'll have to do it yourself or ask one of your siblings. Back in 1999, I left an iron on all day, and the thermostat broke. It overheated and fell on the carpet. That landlord was so mad at me."

Adam cocked his head and crossed his arms. The small, crooked smile was working its way onto his lips. "Go on."

Raquel stopped by the door to her old bedroom. The breath caught in her chest, but she pushed on, turning back to look right at Adam.

"I hate all reptiles. You can never keep them as pets."

Adam laughed. "Deal."

"I don't do vacuuming, weeding, or dusting. That last one isn't because I dislike it; it just makes me cough."

"Okay." His smile grew bigger.

"And I won't allow you to paint the walls in here white. It's just a terrible idea. Makes a house feel like an insane asylum."

"Whatever you say." He put up his hands.

"In short, there are a million reasons I shouldn't stay here. There are a million reasons I'd make a terrible roommate and a terrible girlfriend, and you should send me packing right now."

Raquel put a hand to the doorknob of her old room and turned it. She pushed the door open and stepped inside. The Christmas lights were still in place, still flashing softly and casting a welcoming yellow haze over the room. Raquel turned back to Adam. He was too close behind her, and she nearly knocked into him. She settled for putting a hand to his chest and looking up at his smiling face.

"And worst of all, I'm a terrible slob if you give me the chance to really move into a place," she said. Adam's hands slid around to the small of Raquel's back, pulling her close. The familiar, inviting scent of him made her whole body feel light and airy. "Like, worse than you. Way worse. So last chance. These are all the reasons you don't want me here. And they are way more compelling than the reasons you gave to scare me off from becoming your nurse."

"Is that everything?" Adam asked. One hand worked its way up from her back to slide around and cup her chin, tilting her face closer to his. "Should I remind you of the terrible phone service out here in the boondocks to explain your missed calls, or is this a bad time for that?"

Raquel nodded. The words were all gone. All that rehearsal. All that speech-planning. She was lost in his eyes, in his scent, in his warmth...

"Well then," Adam said with an easy smile. "Sounds like you won't be able to scare me off so easy, Florence. I know what I want. Do you?"

She nodded weakly. Adam pulled her forward and let his lips just graze her own. The touch sent an electric shiver through Raquel's hold body, radiating out through her fingers and toes.

Darn straight, she knew what she wanted. And she was going to take it now.

She grabbed the back of his head, buried her fingers in Adam's thick blonde hair, and pulled him closer. He snorted with laughter before kissing her back and slamming the door behind them with his free hand.

TWENTY-FOUR
SPRING 2002

THE TINY GOLDFINCH chapel looked gorgeous in winter shades of burgundy and navy.

The crowd was of modest size but bursting with energy. Raquel smiled to herself from her spot behind the double doors as she watched Adam's youngest siblings, Jacob and Ruth, taking off the fancy Sunday shoes their parents had made them wear and stashing them under a pew in favor of comfortable socked feet. Abby was sitting in a back row (sans Jude), exchanging what looked like juicy wedding gossip with a local Raquel didn't recognize. Miriam was sitting in a front pew next to Raquel's father; she looked happy and excited, her gardenia corsage fluttering each time she ran a fidgety hand through her long black hair.

"How do I look?" Raquel turned at the sound of Ida's voice.

"Radiant," Raquel replied, tucking a rogue lock of hair back behind her friend's ear.

"You don't think anyone will notice that I'm wearing my kitchen shoes under this dress, do you?" Ida asked, lifting her skirt and shuffling her feet to showcase the black slip-grip tennis shoes she had on.

Raquel laughed and rolled her eyes. "I cannot believe you wore those."

"I've been to a few weddings in my day, love," Ida replied with a smile, eyes sparkling with mischief. "You learn to stay comfortable where you can."

"I think you're safe from scrutiny," Raquel admitted. "Everyone will be too distracted by how gorgeous you look to notice your shoes."

The music shifted, growing louder and slower. The strings positioned at the north end of the chapter started in on an instrumental cover of The Dixie Chicks' *Cowboy Take Me Away*. Raquel thought it sounded like perfection.

"Ready?" Adam appeared by her side, sliding his arm through hers. The first of the small crew of bridesmaids had started their walk down the aisle.

"As I'll ever be," Raquel told him with a smile. She pulled him closer with her hooked arm, enjoying the way that his body felt next to hers.

As the chorus kicked in, they stepped through the double doors, leaving Ida behind them with her elderly father and his walker. One last glance in their direction left Raquel feeling confident that Ida was ready for this—her latest and hopefully final—marriage, comfortable slip-grip shoes and all.

Raquel glanced up at the altar where her abuelo waited with a sappy grin on his face. Diego had fallen for Ida sight unseen. He'd proposed over the phone before he ever even took his first visit out to Goldfinch, and the pair had been inseparable ever since. He seemed so ready now. So eager. Raquel found herself envying his ability to so easily jump into something new. There was a lesson to be learned from him, and she sent up a silent prayer of gratitude now that she had learned from her abuelo sooner rather than later.

She sent a quick glance up at Adam as they took the last few feet of their walk to the altar together. His skin was bright and healthy, a far cry from the clammy blue shade she'd seen at the hospital that awful day months ago. His crooked little smile sent Raquel's belly into delighted tumbles. Lord, he was handsome.

She hated to let him go as they parted ways at the altar. Adam squeezed her hand one more time before releasing it. He bent close to kiss her cheek and whisper "We're next" in her ear before taking his spot. Raquel's smile was so big, it hurt her cheeks.

The ceremony was movie quality. Ida blushed like a schoolgirl when she said "I do." Diego had pulled her into the lap of his wheelchair for their first kiss, sending the audience into roaring laughter as her gartered leg kicked up into the air. The black slip-grip shoes were on full display, but not a soul seemed to mind. After, the goofy tune to the Beatle's *When I'm Sixty-Four* rang through the chapel as the wedding party exited to attend the reception. Ida hooted with laughter as Diego took the ramp down with her still on his lap, racing back to the double doors.

Adam found Raquel again, sliding his arm around her shoulders. "I vote that we collect our slices of wedding cake and take them back to the house for a little movie marathon."

She elbowed him playfully. "Come on, I'm Maid of Honor! We can't bail."

"Did you catch the speed on Diego's chair?" Adam asked her, eyes wide. "That man did not look like the kind who was going to hang around his reception making sure the whole wedding party made it in. They're going straight back to Ida's apartment to break in the new furniture set we all got them. Guaranteed."

"Oh, geez, gross!" Raquel gagged. "That's my grandfather!"

They were interrupted by Adam's brother, Matthew, who had slid up to them looking preoccupied and excited. "Hey, did you guys get introduced to that blonde bridesmaid over there?" He asked them, eyes glued on a tall, thin girl taking off her wedding heels.

"Ida's niece?" Raquel asked him with a chuckle. "Matty, April is a professional model back in New York. Don't you think she's a little—"

"My type?" Matthew supplied, straightening his tie as he only half-listened to Raquel. He licked his thumb and smoothed back the front of his hair. It immediately *boing*ed back into its signature cowlick despite the effort. "I'm about to ask out my future girlfriend, guys. Wish me luck."

Raquel started to protest, but Adam squeezed her hand, stopping her. "Good luck, Matty," he said with a laugh as his brother took off to face sure rejection.

"Is that really the best idea?" Raquel asked Adam, one eyebrow raised.

"Hey, don't kill his spirit," Adam smiled down at her. "I know from experience what it's like to go after a girl who's way out of your league." He winked.

Adam took Raquel's hand, and they started back down the aisle. They pushed through the double doors, happy sounds from the reception just down the hall echoing around the church foyer.

"I'll admit that Matthew's been on kind of a feeding frenzy lately," Adam said with a laugh. "He's asked me if you have any sisters more than once."

"Well, color me flattered," she replied.

"I worry about him sometimes," Adam said, his eyes looking just a little far away as he considered his younger brother. "He's got the opposite problem from what I had: too much cockiness, not enough happiness in what he's got. I wish he'd just find a nice girl and settle down all ready."

"He'll figure it out," Raquel assured him.

They entered the reception hall, where more country music was blaring over the loudspeakers. Miriam walked over to them, plates in hand. She was shaking her head as though she couldn't decide what to do with her face.

"Your grandfather bailed on his own reception," she informed her daughter. "Those two took the wedding car before your cousin Mikey could even decorate it!"

Adam laughed out loud. Raquel elbowed him in the side, suppressing her own smile.

"Want some ice cream?" Miriam asked them. "They're cutting the cake already. No use in waiting if Dad and Ida are already gone."

She held out the plates. Raquel had a sudden, vibrant flashback to another ice cream encounter. Melted rocky road. Hard tile floors. Labored breathing.

Raquel took the plate and plucked a plastic spoon out of her mother's hand.

"Sounds perfect," she announced before spooning up a bite and swallowing it down.

Raquel grinned, sure that there were chocolate pieces stuck between her teeth. She didn't care. How could she when this handsome, funny, determined, *perfect* cowboy was standing next to her, loving her and laughing with her despite all the imperfections?

Raquel knew just what she wanted. And she was beyond grateful that it was hers for the taking.

REVIEW

We hope you've enjoyed Rescue Someone Lonesome, a Sweet Gardner Ranch Western Romance.

If you did, please consider leaving a review on Amazon or Goodreads. Reviews can do so much for up and coming authors and your thoughts would be appreciated.

ABOUT THE AUTHOR

Brittni is up and coming in published fiction, but oh-so-familiar to the pen. An accomplished comedian, writer, and performer, she has delighted audiences for years all over the country.

Now she's bringing her wit and attitude to the printed page with heartfelt, sweet, and raw contemporary romance.

Connect on Facebook to hear the latest about her upcoming books!

Completely Undatable

From the Top

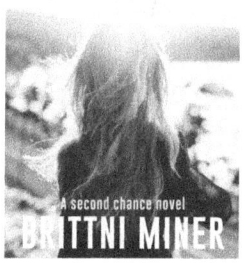

www.ingramcontent.com/pod-product-compliance
Lightning Source LLC
Chambersburg PA
CBHW060928180626
46817CB00004B/1446